THE SECOND GREATEST INEVITABILITY

THE SECOND GREATEST INEVITABILITY

A NOVEL

MICHAEL GRYBOSKI

AMBASSADOR INTERNATIONAL
GREENVILLE, SOUTH CAROLINA & BELFAST, NORTHERN IRELAND

www.ambassador-international.com

THE SECOND GREATEST INEVITABILITY

Paperback ISBN: 978-1-64960-618-1
eISBN: 978-1-64960-669-3

Cover design by Hannah Linder Design
Interior Typesetting by Dentelle Design
Editing by Kate Marlett

Ambassador International titles may be purchased in bulk for education, business, fundraising, or sales promotional use. For information, please email sales@emeraldhouse.com.

AMBASSADOR INTERNATIONAL
Emerald House
411 University Ridge, Suite B14
Greenville, SC 29601
United States
www.ambassador-international.com

AMBASSADOR BOOKS
The Mount
2 Woodstock Link
Belfast, BT6 8DD
Northern Ireland, United Kingdom
www.ambassadormedia.co.uk

The colophon is a trademark of Ambassador, a Christian publishing company.

AUTHOR'S NOTE

For me, it was just another algebra class at Minnie Howard, the ninth grade campus of T.C. Williams High School of Alexandria, Virginia. We did some in-class work; my teacher did his best to drill certain concepts into my head; and then the bell rang.

From there, we students went to our Team Advisory class, a short period of about fifteen minutes that was basically a recess, where we teenagers usually passed the time playing cards. Only this time, on that particular day, we were kept there for about three hours. During the unusually long T.A. period, the office announced over the intercom that there had been attacks on the Twin Towers and the Pentagon.

In the days before smart phones and before most social media platforms were launched, it was easy to keep us in the dark about the specifics. And so, I did not learn the fullest extent of the tragedy until I got home that afternoon. For those of us with conscious memories of 9/11, we remember life before terrorism was on everyone's mind. And over the next couple of decades, we have learned to adapt to such horrible possibilities.

This novel graphically depicts instances of terroristic violence. It is an essential part of the story, as multiple characters play key roles in this disturbing means of warfare and a society learns to live with such a reality.

In contrast to many entertainment programs out there, which seek to glamorize or otherwise positively portray terrorism, this story rightfully depicts it as vile, destructive, and even self-destructive, as seen with one character in particular who repents. I believe this graphic content to be, in its own way, educational and not gratuitous. Sometimes, one must see the horrible to truly understand the nature of evil.

Not All Shall Sleep.

Not All Shall Be Saved.

Not All Shall Be Damned.

Yet All Shall Be . . .

ACT I

Scene 1

Night slowly embraced the city. It glided into the heavens, consuming the entire skyscape. People were given to minute alarm, going about their many affairs as normal while it crawled into their reality. The streetlights automatically switched on, while many people indoors turned on lamps and overheads. Cars and lorries filled the streets with their headlights in the vesper hour. Each building adapted to the loss of the sun in like manner. That way, the denizens were able to view the world around them with only moderate difficulty. Some still struggled, as many edifices remained darkened for want of inhabitants to flip on the incandescents, halogens, and fluorescents.

It was a European metropolis that had every benefit of modern times: paved roads, electricity, fluoridated running water, wireless internet, multiple hospitals stocked with every government-approved drug, plenty of food—both organic and artificial—public and private transportation, white collar jobs, a low poverty rate, and a broad welfare safety net. The city was comprised of many communities, spanning the spectrum on race, ethnicity, religion, age, and other labels. There was mainstream, counter, and multiculture. There were traditionalists, radicals, and those in between.

David could be described as someone who was in between—or, at least, that was how he depicted himself. On so many aspects of life, he was in the middle of categories. He was no longer a young adult, yet not an elderly soul. He was unmarried, yet not unloved. No royal blood within his veins, yet hardly a commoner. David called that place home, even though he was not born amid its forest of buildings. He was a hard worker, yet not someone who slaved away in a mine or a factory for endless hours.

His city bore the marks of civilization. On the west end was a historic university. Centuries in age, the campus surface was a mixture of well-trimmed grass and dark gray cobblestone. Gothic buildings abounded. A large bell tower placed at the center of the educational institute chimed the hours. Small, vaulted churches were found at various points in the city, all subservient to a cathedral established near the old town neighborhood. The largest and oldest of the sanctuaries, its walls had survived the ravages of Viking invasion, Protestant Reformation, Puritan defacing, and several near-misses from bombs dropped during the Second World War. There were also multiple venues for theaters and cinema, a humble professional sports stadium, and a couple dozen schools, some public and some overseen by minority religious sects.

David was among a few hundred thousand who called the community home. While a melting pot, hierarchy still existed. The inner parts of the city were lower class, filling with an ever-growing immigrant population. Blue collar crime was a nuisance, and many tended to avoid the area in the late evenings, unless there were popular citywide events. Guy Fawkes Day was one example, with burning effigies placed all over the quarter. Folks of all backgrounds took part in that festive observance. David himself was known to personally light a couple of the fires, much to his and his neighbors' amusement. Yet once the figures went afire, he would bashfully step back into the crowds.

Farther outwards from the urban core, the middling folk made their lot. Some lived in apartments, others in houses surrounded by black iron gates with pointed finials. These were the office workers, government employees, regulators, accountants, and other professionals. They wore ties and pantsuits to work, betted on stocks, sent their children to public schools, and had the occasional holiday away from the neighborhood. Most were native born and Anglo-Saxon, with a birth rate below that of their foreign-born peers. Nearly all had a Christian background, though few of them kept up the practice in adulthood beyond the major holy days. They engaged in cultural activities high and low, reverently sitting in the theater one night, then shouting profanities during a rugby match the next.

Then, there were the higher classes. It is important to first describe them by what they are not. While often mingling with them, these people were not the landed gentry, or as sometimes called, "old money." Such a sapphire-veined community did not reside in the city, even if they periodically graced it. Their domiciles were on grand estates, tracts of land covering much rural territory. Descended from privilege, they were above such fancies as barbaric sports like football or rugby, contenting themselves with cricket, polo, racing, fencing, golf, chess, and backgammon. They were elites who either served in Parliament or lobbied them, who formed their own clubs and took pride in their lineage, with many being able to trace their ancestry to the victors of the Battle of Hastings.

Rather than be among the caste that critics labeled stuffy and snooty, this "new money" was more commendable to the typical commoner. Most started out meager only to rise through conditions to become a venerable lot. To be sure, their beginnings usually derived from middle or upper middle. They were the successful businessmen, investors, and high-ranking professionals. Some were Anglican clergy who may have started higher in society but, for spiritual focus, moved down. Others were immigrants who made it out of the inner city. Still others were foreigners who were fairly wealthy to begin with and simply struggled to transfer their wealth to their new homeland. Many were American; expatriates who came to the city for education or a job or to flee what they viewed as a society gone mad. Unlike the gentry folk, these rising and arriving members of the upper end of the culture varied in their racial, ethnic, and religious origins.

They were not always privy to the proper mannerisms of high society, nor were they always so awkward in their formalities as to be despised. Theirs was a balance. Yet these novel traits were still in good taste. Their choice of dwellings reflected this intermediary status between plebian and patrician. The majority lived on the edges of the city, typically in higher quality apartments. Some owned houses, usually ones with decent décor and either a Georgian or Victorian layout. The preference was for the suite. For those seeking to achieve self-actualization, such sizable quarters allowed for many ways to fashion a unique identity, befitting their chosen preferences.

David was a member of this class. He lived in a penthouse apartment on the northern end of the city. A two-story complex, he was one of only four tenants and the one with the largest flat in the cubic building. Corinthian columns were carved into the four corners of the structure. The main entrance was a large door with a pointed archway. While the corners were carved of stone, the sides of the building were brick, with rectangular windows placed on the walls of both floors. The structure stood between two other apartment complexes on that city block. A minor road dead-ended into another street that ran in front of the main entrance. Retail stores and tea houses populated the two blocks on either side of the minor road. The area was visible in the evening through city lights.

Within the penthouse were many rooms. The largest was the recreation chamber, which was often used for social gatherings. It had six doors leading into it at various points along a narrow hallway that twisted along the apartment interior. The fourth side of the recreation room was a wall with two windows that showed the outside. A multipurpose room, that evening it had a wood-paneled dance floor set in the center. Several small tables, each with a team of chairs, were placed around the edges of the room. On the northern side of the paneling was a short, black platform reserved for the musicians.

To enter the recreation quarters, however, one first had to go through the only entrance to the penthouse. This led to the study room. Adorned in a manner similar to the library that was located elsewhere in the suite, the study's walls were covered with book shelves containing many an intelligent opus, both fiction and nonfiction. Unlike the library, the study also included two ornately carved sideboards that stored several bottles of fine red wine and various glassware. The white wine was stored in a refrigerator in the kitchen, which was strangely placed on one side of the study while the formal dining room was placed on the other. This meant meals cooked in the kitchen took that much longer to arrive to the dining room. The kitchen also lacked an external entrance. This was because the previous resident, who also owned the building, moved the kitchen to a different chamber and had the former route walled up. Other rooms of note—such as the office, the master bedroom, the guest bedroom, and the three bathrooms—were located elsewhere in the large suite.

David was in the study. It was his favorite room. He viewed the library more for storage of books than a place to spend long hours inside. The office was a necessity, the space which held the television he watched only for news and sophisticated performances on the publicly-funded channels. Not one who partook in social media, David had no laptop or smartphone. Once outside of that room, the rest of the penthouse seemed more twentieth century or earlier in its living standard.

David was alone when day became night. He purposely overslept, not leaving his bedroom until the lunch hour. This was his habit whenever he was to host an evening party, as it helped to keep his energy up. After some afternoon time of ease, he set to preparing things. He showered and shaved a second time to be more clean-cut and donned formal attire. For his audience, he chose to wear a white button-up shirt, navy blue dinner jacket and tie, and light-hued khakis, along with black socks and black Oxford shoes. He waited, facing away from the entrance, hands placed on a small wooden table, one of two in the study. Looking outward, contemplative, he uttered aloud a thought.

"The wondrously awful things a man can get away with simply by using the right euphemisms," he pondered aloud, smiling in connivance before a knock at the door disrupted his thinking. "One moment. I'm coming!"

The knocking halted at his behest as he walked toward the polished wooden door. He unlatched the two bolts and then turned the knob, pulling away the thick oak barrier to reveal the help. There were five of them. An older man, shorter than the others, was the boss. The other four people were behind him, each bearing some delectable items for the evening party. David was at ease, as these personnel had serviced his past festivities. Each of the lowly figures felt a warmth of welcome on that cold night.

"Good, glad you made it. And quite early, I see. Come on in," said David as he pulled the door back, standing beside it with an outstretched arm directing the workers into the space.

"Good evening, Mr. al-Nassery," stated the boss. "It's a pleasure to once again serve a party at your flat."

"Thank you, George," replied David while the help put away the first boxes of food and water for the party. Returning from the kitchen through the door that connected it and the study, they veered right to exit the apartment. They descended the stairway to bring up more supplies. "And let me offer my dearest apologies for the situation regarding the lift. It just started malfunctioning this morning."

"No problem, Mr. al-Nassery. As I mentioned over the phone, this block of flats is not the most imposing mountain to scale."

"Thank you, again."

"No problem at all, Mr. al-Nassery," replied George as his employees came up with more supplies. Soon enough, they had taken up all that was necessary and worked to prepare the cuisine for the event.

For David, it was an event with an agenda buried among the covers of festivity and sophistication.

Scene 2

As the night rose, the temperatures fell. Breath became visible in the outdoors. Arms required covering to achieve comfort. It was not a harsh climate given to blizzards, tundra, or Polar Vortexes. A gulf stream that surged from the Atlantic prevented the island nation from receiving the level of frigidity given to other nations at that line of latitude. Snow was not common. Still, vesper hours were capable of cold. This was especially so for that time of year, with the daylight hours decreasing.

Both Michael Bradford and his wife, Megan, were prepared for the chilly forecast. An overcoat covered his dinner jacket. Each had graying hair and decades of adulthood to their credit. She had a winter jacket and also a shawl covering her arms. Stockings under the flowing dress also helped Megan retain heat while they walked from a nearby car garage. It was after supper, and most of the shops on either side of the street were closed. One tea house that was scantily occupied remained open but not for long. Michael turned to look into the windowed wall and saw a young man somberly looking down at his cup, a brown fedora placed on the table with a brown jacket draped over the chair.

"We're early," said Megan, looking at her smartphone. "I told you we didn't need to leave so early."

"Now, now, Meg," replied Michael with a raised finger, "there was always a chance that traffic was going to rule against us. Besides, David expects us to come early."

"Are you sure?" she asked as they stopped in front of the street between them and the apartment complex main entrance. A driver who had been patiently waiting at the stop sign was just starting to move his vehicle. The Bradfords stood a few feet away from the edge of the sidewalk while the car drove by.

"Positive," he said with his usual confidence.

His was an airy optimism that bordered on the arrogant yet somehow never traversed into the territory. Coupled with his dashing smile, Megan was reminded of why she fell for this man decades ago while studying at the university. The way he debated with the philosophy majors impressed her also. Michael never took one of their courses for his degree and thus came to their dialogues with an amateur background. Yet he seemed able to play havoc with their viewpoints. She found the whole exercise entertaining; and from there, romance bloomed with outstretched petals.

After crossing the street, they came to the front of the complex, where the entrance door had a stopper in place to keep it from closing, giving a view of the indoor ascending staircase. The help placed the hard object there because the main door always locked upon shutting. The stopper also benefitted the guests and musical ensemble.

While the opening was just wide enough for two people to enter at once, Michael stepped to the side and, with a smile, let his wife enter first.

Megan gave him a wry smile in response, the two again beside each other as they ventured up the stairs, the broken elevator to their left.

"You know, I think this is the first time you have met David."

"I think you're correct," Megan replied. "What's he like?"

"Hard to describe him so succinctly."

The two ascended the carpeted, clean stairs of the narrow hallway. Michael grasped the railing on the left as he ascended the climb with his wife. After several steps, the two came upon a landing that went for six feet before terminating. The railings on either side stopped for that flat stretch but then continued with the next set of stairs.

"You can try, can't you?"

"Why, yes, I will." Michael took to the next group of stairs with Megan close behind. "He is kind, sophisticated, sociable to the point of being bubbly. Philosophically, he is a seeker like myself, aware of the powers beyond our immediate environment yet hesitant to pick a specific team. He is learned, literary, and classical."

"I heard he does human rights work."

"Some, yes. Mostly focused on his homeland."

"Where is that?"

"The 'Bible lands,' as they used to call them."

"Ah, I see," said Megan as the two reached the floor of David's penthouse flat. In front of them was the door to the apartment. To their left were the gray doors of the broken elevator. To their right was a long line of brass coat hangers. Above the hooks was a wooden shelf where people were expected to place hats. The Bradfords hung their jackets with care, picking the hooks closest to the penthouse entrance so that it was easier to recount their location later. "He must have seen a lot violent stuff growing up, yes?"

"Yes, Meg, he did," replied Michael as he opened the door for his wife. Unlike the main entrance, the apartment door could be made to stay unlocked upon closing. The door had two latches, plus a key hole for a third level of protection. Michael had learned these intricacies during past visits to David's apartment.

Upon entering the study, they saw a couple of the hired help double-checking things, as the party had not yet officially begun. The Bradfords entered, creating little disruption. Michael quickly spotted David, whose back was to them. He was speaking with the lead singer and the conductor for the ensemble. The other members of the entertainment were setting things up in the recreation room. While unable to make out the exact quotes of the conversation, the Bradfords observed the warm facial expressions and the gentle tone of those involved. After the trio laughed, the singer and her conductor exited the study to go to join the rest of the ensemble. David turned around to see Michael and Megan, the host welling with happiness at their arrival.

"Ah, Michael Bradford," he said as he approached his guest, shaking his hand. "My favorite philosopher. How goes it, good sir?"

"Quite well, David. Quite well."

"And this must be Megan Bradford," said David, turning his attention to her. At the extension of her hand, he took hold of it and kissed it. "A pleasure to finally meet you. Michael told me you were as radiant on the inside as you are on the outside. And he told no lie."

"You're too kind, Mr. al-Nassery," Megan responded.

"Did you have any delays in your journey? I usually expect you earlier than this," said David with a smile.

"Meg here thought it best to be fashionably early," said Michael, with all three laughing at the concept.

"Well, then," David noted aloud, "as the honorary first guests to arrive, you get the award of trying out a new wine I recently procured."

David motioned for them to follow him across the study, where the sideboard with the red wine was located.

"Pardon me for my ignorance," began Megan, "but I thought Muslims were not allowed to drink."

"You are correct; they do not," replied David as he opened the sideboard and took out a bottle of the crimson liquid.

"Oh, my apologies."

"Quite all right. It is a common mistake."

"Oh, it's not just that. My husband told me in advance that you were a seeker."

"Truly," remarked David as he handed the bottle to one of the hired help standing nearby. "And while I still seek, I do concur with what that great American theologian Benjamin Franklin once said." The help popped open the dark green bottle without incident and then handed it back to the host. Setting the opened bottle on the table, David turned to fetch three small glasses from the other sideboard.

"And what would that be?" Megan asked.

"'Wine is constant proof that God loves us,'" recited David, eliciting smiles from the Bradfords. Pouring a small sampling of the potent contents into each glass, he gave one to each guest. Then he took hold of one glass with his left hand while placing the bottle down on one of the two small wooden tables. "What shall we drink to?"

"Health, friends, and what I venture to think shall be a smashing party," stated Michael.

David nodded as the three each took to gently swirling their glasses.

Lifting the items to their noses, they inhaled the aroma before sipping their drinks. Midway through the small imbibing, simple musical tones were heard through the two walls that separated the study from the recreation chamber. The wine glasses all empty, the three savored the taste of the fine spirit within them before returning to conversation.

"A good toast and a good drink," David concluded.

"Quite so, David," Megan agreed.

"Did we just have the famous Chaldean wine I have heard so much about?"

"Oh, no, no." David gently rebuffed. "That will be enjoyed after the party begins. There are only so many privileges with being first."

"Indeed." Michael said, laughing. "So, what did we consume?"

"Just a regular red brew from the mainland. You know, a French provincial one that mixes grapes and spices to provide a nice peppery finish."

"That is how I felt. A respectable vintage," Megan said.

"Though I will say with grand confidence, Meg, that the best of the fermented pleasures is that precious drink from my friend's home country," Michael claimed.

"They make wine in your homeland?" she asked.

"They used to. Thankfully, I found myself in possession of a fair stock of bottles. The more they are consumed, the rarer and more valuable they become."

"Dare I say, Mr. al-Nassery, that perchance you should consider halting your consumption, lest you run out?"

"Now, now, Mrs. Bradford," commented David. "A fine wine is like a fine life. Though it eventually is finished, the enjoyment it spreads to others will never be forgot."

"Quite the philosophical declaration. What writer came up with such a clever preponderance?"

"Well," David said with a faint blush, "I did, actually." The three laughed at the impromptu genius of their host as the door opened with more guests arriving.

Scene 3

"Ah, the Right Honorable Charles Harrison," exclaimed David as the middle-aged politician entered the study. Harrison grinned and the two shook hands.

"A pleasure seeing you again, Mr. al-Nassery."

"Likewise, likewise."

"Let me begin by informing you that my wife Ava gives her regards; but unfortunately, she cannot make it."

"Oh, a pity. Is she ill?"

"Hardly, David. When we got word that the lift was broken, that was all she wrote, as they say. As you know, Ava is not a big fan of stairs."

"Well, I do apologize for that. The malfunction was very last minute and very annoying."

"No problem at all," said Harrison lightheartedly. "It was hardly your fault. Besides, unlike my wife, I am all right with stairs."

"Well, in that case, the next time I invite you, I will be sure to again sabotage the device," David quipped, his distinguished guest guffawing briefly. Through the walls, the two men heard the noises of festivity. In the recreation room, most of the guests were already present. Light refreshments were served. Instrumental music filled the space.

Harrison slowly walked around the study, admiring the many books that crowded the shelves. The many spines displayed names like Faulkner, Poe, Shakespeare, Byron, Tennyson, Orwell, Weisel, King, and many others of the great Western literati pantheon.

David changed the topic. "How go the corridors of power?"

"The usual. Not much is happening these days, what with the Christmas recess and all," replied Harrison with his arms behind his back. "You want to talk business at this hour?"

"Even later, actually," said David as he put his hand on Charles' shoulder. "After the party dies down, I would like to review the bill before you opt to file it for next session."

"By all means."

"Anyway, until then"—David patted Charles' back—"feel free to enjoy your surroundings. The wine, the song—not so much the women, lest Ava and the free press hear about it."

"Yes, quite the warning," said Harrison with an amused and stuffy laugh. From there, the distinguished guest exited the study and ventured to the epicenter of the party.

After the member of Parliament left the room, David paced a few times before approaching George. The head of the help, he was standing loyally by, occasionally directing the traffic of experienced servants and professional cooks.

"George," said David as he walked up to him, taking a place near the study door that led into the kitchen.

"Yes, Mr. al-Nassery?"

"With Mr. Harrison's arrival, I do not believe many guests are still pending."

"I think you are right, Mr. al-Nassery. By my count, there probably aren't more than two or three people, maybe four or five."

"And they might have decided to not show up because of the lift problem. So could you please mind the door and welcome anyone who may show up late?"

"That I shall."

"Good, because I need to make the rounds. You know, 'work the room,' as some folks say. Also, I think there will be speeches."

"Understood, Mr. al-Nassery."

"Do you have the guest list handy?"

"Yes, I do, right here." George took from his pocket a smartphone that, after a couple taps, revealed all the names for the party. David smiled.

"You know, back in my day, we used a clipboard and paper," David quipped, fully aware that George was several years older than he.

With a pat on George's shoulder, David turned away and opened the door leading to the hallway. It was slightly narrower than the stairway space that led to his apartment. The party noises became mildly louder. Then, he opened the door in front of him and entered the large indoor space. He was flooded with music and chatter, happiness, and decorum. Guests wore formal attire. Some of the men wore bowties; others had ties. Dinner jackets were common. Women wore flowing dresses, and some wore high heels. The ensemble was still playing slow melodies. The singers had yet to sing their first bars, and the more elegant numbers remained to be performed. As David entered the recreation room, he found a cluster of guests that included the Bradfords. He smiled when he came within earshot of the words uttered, as it was clear that Michael was again debating.

"And I would like to point out that there are indications of a life beyond this one," explained Michael, his wife by his side. He was countering the remarks of a man half his age who was standing on the opposite side of the circled group of partiers. "Consider the countless instances of out-of-body experiences, near death experiences. There are plenty of people, regardless of spiritual views, who have been clinically brain dead and yet were able to give details on what happened in the room. Surely, this shows that the mind and the brain can be separate. Thus, a mind can endure after a body has decayed."

"I can see your point," conceded the youth, a recent graduate from the same university the Bradfords attended. "But maybe these were merely special incidents. You know, an even deeper part of the brain's operations. I know the latest scholarship states that near-death experiences are probably just extreme adaptions by the brain in response to traumatic physical injuries, like going to one's 'happy place,' except on steroids."

"A steroid-induced happy place, this is becoming an interesting conversation," interjected David, turning the group's attention to himself.

"It was interesting before that, you know," said Megan.

"Is my good, old philosopher friend causing more trouble at one of my parties?" David inquired playfully.

"Hardly—no offense taken," said the young man, getting a couple of nods from the others in the group, attesting to his honesty. "I quite like such conversations. In college, they do not always feel comfortable bantering about such sensitive matters."

"He has a fine mind, my son Oliver," said Fennimore Wellington, an older gentry figure whose wife was socializing with their lady friends across the room.

"That is universally agreed upon," added Michael.

"All right, just making sure nothing too provocative was coming to pass. I long for the breaking of bread, not of bones," noted David, getting smiles and quick spurts of laughter. "Carry on, carry on."

David continued to go about the groups of talkers and revelers, civilized in their garb and lecture, composed even as they consumed a choice vintage from his homeland. Mingling with the clusters of guests was the help. Both men and women who served those present wore a uniform consisting of a white collared button-up shirt, a black bowtie, black pants, black shoes, and black sleeveless vests with brass buttons going down the center. They balanced fiberglass serving trays that featured an assortment of finger foods. Finely decorated, tasty morsels were picked off as servants walked through high society. More food was set up in the dining room on the main table. Along the tabletop were multiple chafers with roll-tops, some of which had two open fuel holders underneath their frame to keep their respective cuisine warm. Items in the chafers or gathered on the trays included shrimps with cocktail sauce, strips of lamb, garlic bread, penne, and, for the sweet-toothed, a diverse assortment of dark chocolate treats. Toothpicks and clear plastic plates were readily available.

While many of the servers provided food, others went around the social groups to provide the drinks. They came with silver serving trays and included items with and without alcohol. Clear, plastic cups a few inches tall were used for the water and the soda. Each of these liquid containers had its share of ice cubes taking up space. The wines provided for the evening were scarlet in color, and the glassware used had a tall stem and broad bowl. This aided in granting sufficient access to the aroma of the substance, which was crafted from overseas and shipped in by the host. While a few of the wines offered hailed from mainland Europe, the favorite breed was from the Middle East.

"David, David!" shouted a gentleman behind. He was quick to turn and greet the man, whom he had exchanged quick pleasantries with when he first arrived.

"Cyril Williams, MP," the host replied, grinning. "Is there a problem?"

"Only if you get stage fright easily," replied Williams.

With an arm around David's shoulders and another arm pointing the way, the two men went to the center of the dance floor. It was empty. The crowd of guests had their social circles gathered around the other parts of the large room. Before the two men was a microphone attached to a stand. It was one of the devices that the ensemble was going to use later.

Williams tapped on the end of the microphone, the thuds echoing throughout the enclosed space. "Attention, everyone. Attention. Can I please have everyone's attention?"

Guests gravitated toward the center of the dance floor. Some were near enough to simply turn around. Others walked with expedience. A few were at the circular tables placed in the room on three sides of the dance floor. They rose and joined the others, whose various conversations quieted. Most of the help stayed to the peripheries. A couple of the uniformed servants still made rounds, just in case an empty glass needed refilling or a plastic plate needed removal.

"Excellent," Williams observed aloud before continuing. "Good evening, everyone. I am the Right Honorable Cyril Michael Williams. While I am not an official organizer of this splendid social occasion, I still felt it mandatory to offer a few words before going any further in our beloved festivities. As some of you know, I have always been a man of privilege. My father, like myself, served in Parliament and so did his father before him. I come from a long line of wealthy, elder statesmen. So I have never known what it is like to be in want. Therefore, I always hold great respect for anyone who can rise up from less advantageous circumstances and become a fine member of elite society."

David stood beside Cyril, patiently smiling with his hands held together as he knew what was coming next.

"Our dear and generous host is one such example—and a splendid example, at that. I do not know how many are aware of this, but the other day marked exactly ten years since Mr. David al-Nassery came to our beloved island. With little to his possessions, he worked hard and bet savvy all the while charming us into submission. I myself met David seven years ago at a Boxing Day party. The man is full of mirth, intellect, and culture. Beyond that, he is also a man who cares about his homeland and the less fortunate. A charitable soul, a cultured soul, and a witty mind, David, I am pleased to call you friend." Applause followed the remarks, with Williams and David shaking hands.

After David stepped back from Williams and the microphone, the member of Parliament continued. "And now, if it would not be too much trouble, I think I speak for the entirety of this room when I say that it would be an honor to hear a few words from our host."

More applause and even some cheering. The enthusiasm was too notable to be rejected. Mouthing the words "well, if I must," David approached the microphone and shook Williams' hand once more. This time, it was the Parliament member who took a few steps back and gave the host the floor. David looked over the semicircle of interested people. They were elegant and attentive, offering kind gazes and full focus. With a great smile, David addressed the audience of eager company.

"Thank you, Right Honorable Williams, for your kind words. Thank you, servers, for once again making civilized life possible for the rest of us. And thank you, each of you, my friends and friends of friends, for coming tonight. I believe it was that Bard of Avon who stated that 'if music be the food of love, play on.' The merriment will continue soon enough, the thrills of this proper evening will remerge eventually. Until then, I give my own little notice of the ending of 'the winter of our discontent.'

"When I first came to your country, I was quite frightened. I know recent political developments lead many to not look fondly upon the foreigner, much less one from my background. And yet, how could I forget that England is the most civilized country on earth . . . except when it comes to football, of course."

David paused while most of his guests laughed and nearly all the rest grinned. "At every point, I was given opportunity. At every juncture, a mercy here and there. I am here because of you. I have succeeded because you, gentry and commoner alike, gave me the chance to be something. Be it good, old Michael Bradford giving me a post at his bookstore or good Fennimore Wellington taking me on to oversee his winery and, of course, to prevent him from drinking all of it . . . " Another pause filled with laughter. "The important point is that your charity is the reason I am here.

"I have told many of you my share of stories from the old country. It is not a pleasant place. My hometown remains under a cruel and brutal occupation. It will always trouble me that I had to run away, to flee like a coward. I wanted to fight; but at the same time, I knew it would be a quixotic adventure—at most optimistic. They have the big guns, the military budget, the supplies, the sympathy from many people—especially from across the pond—and the media. What do my people have? Hopefully, before too long, they will have your government. They will be aided by you with the same compassion with which you aided me."

A solemn moment passed while David allowed for the profound comment to manifest within his company. Then, a slow but powerful applause was given. Smiling with his head bowed, David concluded after the claps ebbed away.

"Well, with that being noted, let us continue our festivities. This floor was meant for dancing; and while I am not much for that myself, I am sure everyone else here is. So since music is the food of love, I say, play on!"

Williams rushed to the microphone. "Not so fast, there David. We are not going to do any of that until you get a well-deserved toast. Does everyone have a drink?" Some yeses were given from the crowd. Those who remained silent were in agreement. Williams was the only one lacking a drink, but a member of the help immediately solved that problem. "Very good, then, let me offer a toast to you."

Williams raised his glass, and the other guests followed his example. David was a couple of steps removed from the microphone and stood there, trying to be bashful. Williams was closer to the microphone, making sure that all in the space were capable of hearing his words. "To Mr. David al-Nassery. Philanthropist, intellectual, and a very good friend. Long may you live. Cheers!"

"Cheers!" responded most of the guests as they lifted their glasses a little bit higher with the exclamation and then drank the contents.

"I'm not blushing, am I?" asked David lightheartedly, garnering amused laughter from Williams and most of the guests standing nearby.

"No, no; you're all right," assured Williams.

"Now, can we continue the party?" asked David with a smile, his words mostly amplified by the microphone beside him.

"By all means," replied Williams, with another spontaneous applause rendered by the guests before the microphone was carried back to the ensemble and the two men exited the dance floor.

SCENE 4

Guests danced to the melodies, inspired by their passion and the beats. The soprano of the ensemble led the vocals. Her voice perfectly struck each note, no matter how fast or high. She was a professional, having plied her auditory craft in concert halls across the western world. Around her was a small orchestra fashioned in the Baroque style. Instruments in the ensemble included a lute, a hammered dulcimer, stringed instruments, a harp, and a bagpiper. Each knew their parts and had sheet music to guide their ways. Each number was rapid and at times extended for longer dances. When a selection was concluded, the dancing ceased and the audience applauded.

Songs played for the energetic guests featured a fusion of Celtic folk, vespers, pre-Christian British, and even Medieval monastic chants. Many of the numbers were part of the ensemble's Christmas offerings. Those active inhabitants of the paneled floor performed a myriad of dance moves in response to the rhythms, from the traditional to the contemporary. Many danced face-to-face, each with their arms behind their backs while kicking their legs up and stomping them down. Couples held hands, swaying their bodies to the patterns of notes. Some quit after a few songs.

Others joined late. A few were avid enough to maintain a presence for most of the performances.

Three friends were on break from the dance floor. Each took a seat at a rounded table. They were the only ones at that part of the recreation room. All three of them were women who had worked their way up to high society. It was through mutual employment that they met. The youngest was Piper. A red-haired lass from Dublin, she had graduated from Trinity College the year before. She had opted to move to the United Kingdom for better economic opportunity. Seated to her left was Amelia. A fair-skinned blonde, she had just turned thirty and was the tallest of the friends. The eldest was Elizabeth. She had brown hair with a hint of blonde and sea green eyes. Each one was drinking from a glass of freshly poured wine, specifically the preferred brand of David. They were talking, laughing, listening to the music, and watching the actions of the dance floor.

"You really should read the book," said Piper to Amelia. "It's a real page-turner. I'm a hundred pages in and still haven't found a dull moment."

"But I cannot make it to book club."

"I know, I know, so you say," conceded Piper. "You could still read it on your free time. You're always telling me you want something to pass the time in the cubicle."

"There is that. All right, sure. It's at the library, right?"

"We wouldn't have selected it if it wasn't. You know how that group is; either they're really thrifty or really poor. Or poormouthing, come to think of it."

"Which is another reason why I don't bother with them," noted Amelia, who sipped some wine before continuing. "There aren't any good men there, I bet."

"Shapers and chancers. Little else."

"But maybe a man that our spinster friend here might want. Right, Lizzie?"

Elizabeth was not paying heed to the words of her friends. She was smirking, staring forward beyond the faces of her companions.

"Lizzie? Lizzie!"

"Yes, what is it?" she asked Amelia, maintaining her gaze away from her friends at the table. "Something about a book club, right?"

"Yes," said Piper. "Amelia and I think you might want to go to book club. There might be a man there to your liking."

"Why bother when the man I want is here?" she asked without looking at her friends. The two women turned their attention to what Elizabeth was captivated by. The two were stunned and impressed all at once.

"You mean . . . David al-Nassery?" asked Piper.

"Yes."

"Good luck, my dear," said Amelia. "The man is a bachelor through and through. He has never been seen in the company of a woman."

"That is because he has never seen me."

"He's met you, you langered soul," Piper commented critically.

"When?" asked Elizabeth, whose shock at the statement finally broke their focus on the sociable David.

"Remember that Cavalier descendants brunch my boyfriend invited us to last month?"

"Vaguely."

"He was there."

"That does not count," she firmly stated. "He was busy with the others. We exchanged simple greetings and nothing more."

"Were you smitten with him then?"

"Quite smitten," declared Elizabeth, who then finished her wine. "And I will get to him in a way that no woman has ever tried to do."

"And how would that be?"

"Simple, dearest Piper. I will get him to dance with me."

 Both of her friends laughed.

"Good one."

"Very funny."

"What?" she asked in disbelief. "He is able."

"He doesn't dance," stated Amelia.

"My, my, you can be cheeky."

"I'm not being cheeky. I am being honest," Amelia replied. "In all the social events I have seen him attend, never have I seen him dance."

"Might be a religious thing," Piper interjected.

"He's not Muslim, dearest Piper."

"Be that as it may, Liz, you will not get him to a dance."

"Prepare to be wrong, my dears," said Elizabeth with a confident smile as she stood from her chair and walked toward her target.

David was socializing with Parliament members Charles Harrison and Cyril Williams, as well as Oliver Wellington. Fennimore Wellington was elsewhere, having had yet another glass of wine. Unaware of the conversation between the three female friends in the corner of the recreation room, the men continued to lightly banter as the music brought energy on the paneled wooden floor. The two Parliament members held wine glasses by their stems, occasionally sipping the contents. The younger Wellington held a plastic cup of soda with ice. The elected officials stood side-by-side facing opposite Oliver, while David was the keystone completing the U-shape.

"So, how was the match in question?"

"Such curiosity, as though he had never seen the Yanks play on the telly," commented Harrison in response to David's query.

"As a matter of fact, I haven't," David replied, grinning.

"Of course not," replied Harrison with questionable sincerity. "Anyway, the game was an interesting one. Their version of football is far more militaristic. They don armor and helmets, charge and Blitz, collide and clash."

"Brute savagery, if you want my opinion," interjected Williams.

"Oh, come, I have seen the same sport; and I think their football has much in the line of strategy, tactics, psychology," responded Oliver.

"Admittedly, they have a pinch of such higher tendencies. Still, I say, they lack the civilized interaction, the meticulous processes, and the coordinated discernment one finds with a good match of our football."

"Our football is boring," declared Oliver, nearly driving Williams to spit out his wine while eliciting a laugh from David. "Well, it is. At least the Yanks' football brings the drive and the excitement of a grand struggle."

"Such horrid thoughts."

"Now, now, good Cyril," said David, giving a pat on the shoulder of Oliver, "a contrarian mind is a mind at work."

Oliver smiled at the compliment while the two elected officials tacitly pondered the remark. Before either was able to offer a rebuttal, an older gentleman entered the room and rushed to the meet the four men. He was a guest at the party and, until then, had been enjoying his time. However, upon meeting the four men, he was given to an exasperated mental state.

"Is there a problem, Cedric?" asked David.

"I am dreadfully sorry to interrupt, but I can't seem to get the bill to print out on your computer. I am frightened that it might be lost in the system."

"Hmmm." David pondered. "Did you try unplugging then re-plugging the printer?"

"Yes."

"How about shutting it down and restarting the computer?"

"No need for that, Oliver. I may be ignorant of modern technology; but I know enough to know that the problem is with the document, not the computer."

"It might be a formatting issue," posited Oliver. "Did the computer say anything about the attached document not being the correct format?"

"Well," thought Cedric aloud, "I do seem to recall it said something about the need to convert the files into something else. Is that what you are talking about?"

"Yes, exactly."

"Right, good," said a partially relieved Cedric. "Can you fix it?"

"All you need to do is forward me the email. I should have the right document format on my laptop. From there, I will convert it to something more basic and resend it back to you."

"Your laptop? Did you bring it with you?"

"It's in the boot of my car, which is parked a couple of blocks away from this very flat. Meet me in David's office in about five minutes."

"Right," commented Cedric, now fully relieved. "That sounds like a plan."

"An intelligent mind, indeed," observed David as Oliver exited the chamber to his parked automobile.

"Thankfully, people like him are on our side," said Cedric before nodding and exiting to return to the office room at the other end of the penthouse apartment.

"What's with this whole formats-and-documents situation?" Cyril asked David.

"Above my pay grade, good Cyril," the host replied.

And then, she arrived. David watched Elizabeth walk along the side of the square paneling of the dance floor, careful to not step into the space occupied by avid partiers. Gracefully going amongst the tables, servants, and chatting guests, her movements were also carefully witnessed by Amelia and Piper. They remained seated at the table, exchanging short comments between themselves about her chances, seeming to wonder aloud if a misstep might occur before she even got to address David. No incidents stopped her as she bypassed running into Oliver as he rushed to the exit to get his laptop. She slowed her stride and then stood in proper posture and delightful countenance before the host of the party.

David was surprised by her presence, flinching as though she had attacked him from behind. She seemed very familiar, her sea green eyes, mostly brown hair, and the faint lines along her face harkening him to his past. In a split second, he felt great emotion but, after another moment, realized that she was not the one his memories assumed. Her smile was still captivating, and her eyes still beckoned back to those days. He gave a smile in return as she bowed her head briefly in a greeting.

"You must be Mrs. Elizabeth Florence."

"Miss," she corrected.

"Oh, I see."

"My apologies for not making your acquaintance earlier. By the time my friends and I arrived, a servant had taken over the formal greetings."

"I am sure the pleasure was all his."

"It does not have to be."

"Pardon?"

"I would very much like for you to ask me to dance. That is the proper order of things, unless I am mistaken."

"It is," responded a shifty David. "However, I am not generally one for dancing. Especially this type of music. It is much too fast."

"If I can get them to play something slower, will you ask me for a dance?" countered Elizabeth, her smile weakening but still present.

"Sure," immediately stated David, turning the heads of Harrison and Williams in surprise.

Without hesitation, Elizabeth walked over to the ensemble. The dancing stopped as the participants applauded the latest fast-paced number. Some were growing weary and left the floor for a table. Others meandered around, talking with their dance partners in anticipation for the next song. With opportunity before her, Elizabeth approached the soprano of the ensemble.

David could barely make out what she was saying but knew the gist of her petition. The lead singer nodded and smiled.

The low sounds of minor conversations were evaporated with the clarion call of the bagpipes. A thrust of the instrument drew the attention of the guests and perked up the ears of David. It was a familiar tune, one whose introduction for the cultured man gave away its title and tempo. Elizabeth had quickly convinced the ensemble to pursue a less rapid melody. She returned to face an impressed host.

"Now, will you ask me for a dance, or won't you?" asked the woman, evidently driven by a sense of imminent victory.

David knew when he was beat; he took her right hand with his left. "Good lady," he formally spoke, his eyes locked upon hers, "may I have the pleasure of this dance?"

"Why, yes, kind sir. You may," said Elizabeth with a smile.

While still holding her hand, he went past his pleasantly stunned peers so that he was beside her. They walked side by side through the clusters of guests, each group whispering to another in amazement at what was about to happen. David's refusal to engage in dancing was well known. The floor was cleared of all others, each going to the edge to behold the sight. Another instrument joined the introductory interlude while the two dancers turned to face each other.

David bowed with arms open and one leg stretched forward while Elizabeth curtsied.

A brief pause denoted the end of the interlude as the strings came in with a soprano singing a beautifully haunting text. It was in Gaelic, adding to the sacred mystery of the ancient song. David's left hand and Elizabeth's right gripped again. His other hand wrapped around to touch just above her waist while her left hand wrapped around his upper back. After a few seconds of stillness, a quiet recreation room beholding every moment, the two began to slowly step in good order.

David hid his nervousness well, carefully placing each step while looking into the pleasant face of his dance partner. Elizabeth was more experienced, lacking any visible concern over her own steps.

Their swaying increased as the music included more instruments and the addition of the alto and tenor singers.

Michael and Megan Bradford were standing along the edge of the paneled floor. They had been several feet away from the spot until whispery word spread that David was finally going to dance. David saw the Bradfords take hands and walk beside each other onto the wooden floor, apparently as a way to encourage him. With a bow and a curtsy, the two danced in the same proper manner as David and Elizabeth. While the host and his partner remained near the center of the square floor, the Bradfords remained closer to the edge. Soon after Michael and Megan began to dance, four other couples ventured onto the space and echoed the actions of the first two pairs.

Outside of the apartment complex where the rare occurrence was taking place on the paneled floor, a man waited in the dark. He was in a business casual outfit, with dark gray pants, white button-up collared shirt, and a black tie. To keep warm in the chilly evening, he had on a brown jacket that went a few inches below his waist and a fedora that covered the top of his head. The darkness and the unrevealing attire betrayed his relative youth, clean-shaven face, and black hair. His frame was slim but not skinny, his height slightly above average. His countenance was somber.

The man stood outside of the tea house. It was closed due to the late hour. He studied the apartment complex's main entrance, keeping track of those coming and going. A few others inhabited the sidewalks; however, they kept to themselves. Looking down, he pulled back the brown sleeve of his jacket and then pulled back the white sleeve of his shirt. A digital wristwatch was revealed. He had no phone. With his index finger, he pushed on a small button located on the upper left-hand side of the circular time piece. A bright, neon green light came on, helping him to see the time. Taking a visible deep breath in the thin air, he looked back up at the lights of the penthouse windows. The green glow projected onto his face for a few moments and then evaporated with his exhale.

"You dance beautifully," Elizabeth told David. Her voice was loud enough to be heard by her dance partner, yet soft enough to be lost to the relaxed holy music that enveloped all those within the chamber.

"So do you," responded David, who let loose his right hand from her waist, took a step back, and allowed her to spin before again taking her by the lower back and continuing the gentle stepping. He had spun her twice earlier in the song. Other couples on the floor did likewise at times when they seemed to feel it most appropriate.

As the melody was nearing its conclusion, the soprano coming to her highest yet most profound notes, Elizabeth leaned into David. With a smile and closed eyes, she rested her head on his chest—the show of docile intimacy, the display of faint lustful affection. Her action could only be out of sincere interest.

Yet within David there was tumult. He was returning to what happened, to what occurred years ago and far away. His distraught sentiment came over him, the smile supplanted by grief. She was too similar. Looking up from his dance partner, he saw a dozen faces peering at his every move. Quickly, his grin returned and the audience was none the wiser.

The singers completed their contribution to the piece. Only the strings played the remainder of the song. It was the instrumental signal that all was nearing its conclusion. The various pairs halted their stepping and swaying. Each pair broke away from their grasp and exchanged their bows and curtsies. After the final long note vanished into the past, a thunderous applause was given by the guests. David took hold of Elizabeth's hand as he had when he came upon the dance floor. As everyone directed their admiration toward the center of the space, David laughed it off, quipping "well I try, I try" as he and his female acquaintance walked off the paneled stage.

Scene 5

The man in the fedora looked at his wristwatch again. The green luminance helped him see the time described by the digital Arabic numerals—another deep breath that looked like smoke. Pulling the two sleeves over his wrist, he endeavored for his own sake to not check the time again. The young man knew it was late. He was fairly anxious, yet unafraid. His stomach did not rumble out of fear, nor was he sweating at what he was going to do. Nevertheless, he longed to begin the role so he could be done with the matter. Once it started, he would feel more comfortable. Like he had before. There was no more need to check the time, for he saw them beginning to leave.

"David? David?" a woman interjected. The host turned away from his talk with a couple of members of the retiring ensemble. He found Fennimore Wellington and his wife, arm-in-arm. She seemed to be offering herself as a support beam.

"Ah, Mr. and Mrs. Wellington."

"We just wanted to give our regards for a most wonderful party. Fennimore and I always enjoy these functions."

"And I enjoy that wine of yours," slurred Wellington. He seemed to have most of his wits, but that could only be because of his high tolerance. "Though, I confess, after six helpings, I fear I have forgotten the name of it."

"Chaldean wine," answered David.

"Oh, that's right," he said lightly. "Anyway, good stuff. Well worth the headache tomorrow morning."

"You will see that he gets home safely, yes?" David asked the less drunk of the two.

"Oliver should be driving us once you're done with him," the wife replied.

"That shan't be long," assured David. "As I understand, he has already gotten my printer to do what Cedric tried to do."

"Indeed. Well, tell him we are already making our way down to the automobile."

"I will do so."

"Thank you again, David."

"Yeah, good night and good morning," said Fennimore with a grin as he and his wife turned and then exited the room. David saw them depart, with the husband starting to veer off before his wife clutched him a little harder to keep him on the straight path.

"I hope she can help him with the stairs," quipped Michael Bradford. He, his wife Megan, and David all laughed at the thought.

"Truly, truly."

"Anyway," added Michael, "a good get-together as always. You are an excellent host and a good friend."

"Heading out already? You are usually the last ones to venture away."

"I am feeling a little wearier than usual," stated Megan. "But again, a marvelous party. I should attend your functions more often."

"Indeed," commented David as the Bradfords waved and then followed the Wellingtons out the door of the recreation space.

As the couple departed, David heard Megan comment, "Why did you want me to say that? I don't feel weary at all."

"I'll explain later," came her husband's reply.

Brushing their unusual dialogue off amid more pressing concerns, David became distracted again with wrapping up assorted affairs connected to the party. While a few guests were still meandering, many of the help and the ensemble were packing their things and leaving. Just as he was about to see to other matters pertaining to the closing down of the event, she walked in front of him. Her smile and her eyes drew him in yet again.

"Mr. al-Nassery," Elizabeth spoke in formal tone.

"Miss Florence."

"I enjoyed our dance."

"So did I."

"One of my friends has to work tomorrow. Since I am her ride, I must depart now."

"I am sorry to hear that. I enjoyed your company."

"Can I assume you have my contact information?"

"Yes, I do."

"Then I should expect a phone call from you sometime soon, yes?" asked Elizabeth with wide eyes and a captivating smile.

David smiled back, took her right hand with his left, kissed it, and then slowly let loose, all the while his eyes locked to hers.

Her smile grew with optimism, and then she curtsied while he bowed. Elizabeth then turned to exit, looking back at the host twice before leaving the room.

Before David was able to consume the intimate moment any longer in his mind, business arrived.

"David." Oliver Wellington approached the host, speaking with a formal tone. "I got the bill all printed out. Harrison and Williams have it in the study."

"Very good, very good," replied David. "Your parents are waiting in the car. Feel free to take the rest of the night off."

"You sure I shouldn't double-check with Harrison? I technically work for him, after all."

"I am certain he will not mind. Have a good night, my antithetical friend."

"Good night, David."

The man in the dark knew the number of guests. Keeping track of their coming and going was of great importance. They never beheld him as they departed. Focused on their own pleasures and interests, travels and memories, their eyes did not wander over to his location by the closed teahouse. Even if they directed their ocular organs to behold that area, they would not see much. He stood away from the nearest street lights, confined beside the darkened exteriors of business buildings after hours. His fedora covered much of his head, and the collar of the jacket obscured its share as well. Mouthing the count of people leaving the apartment complex, the young man realized few were left.

With one more deep breath, the vapor gushing upward before dissipating, the man began his determined walk to the apartment complex. The transition from sidewalk to street went without halting as no cars came by. Departing guests paid him scant notice as he walked beside them, going the opposite direction. In good posture, in proper walk, neither noticeably fast nor noticeably slow, he went to the main entrance. The door was still propped open, though the help removed the stopper soon after.

"Those steps were a savage sobriety test," lamented a gentleman, who had just let go of the railing he used to aid his descent.

"All the better that Oliver is driving," replied the woman, about the same advanced age, who gripped him as they continued toward the exit and, from there, to the nearest parking garage.

The young man began his ascent of the staircase. He shifted rightward upon taking the first step, accommodating the trickle of people on the other side. That included a few musicians carrying their instruments. One of them, a woman of about forty with frizzy hair, kept a strong grip on her cello as she neared the bottom floor.

"I told you it was no big challenge," she said to the woman ahead of her, who looked to be part of the same musical troupe. "I've been hauling this mammoth creature around hundreds of times, including flights taller than this."

Behind them descended an older couple. They were the same folks he saw out of the corner of his eye when he was inside the teahouse hours earlier. Because of their early arrival, he had wondered if the party was starting sooner than expected. They briefly looked at the young fellow who was going up the stairs. Theirs was a fleeting curiosity. He also temporarily glanced at them, though he offered nothing further in the form of recognition. Three women, all younger than the couple that had gone before, went down the stairs. Each held onto the railing with one hand and the side of their flowing dresses with the other. Despite the risk of tripping, the front two kept turning their heads to socialize with each other. They arrived at the landing that served at the same time as the young man.

"It's all about strategy," said the woman at the back of the line. "As my dear mum used to say, 'He pursued her until she caught him.'"

"Whatever suits your fancy, Liz," commented the red-haired Irish woman at the front, still with skepticism, despite the unexpected happening of that night.

Continuing up the stairs, the young man shifted more toward the wall on the right side of the narrow passage. This was to make way for two servants, who were carrying empty chafers with sealed shut tops. Just before reaching the top of the second floor, a man younger than he rushed down the steps. Checking his smartphone before beginning his descent, he had his jacket draped over his left arm. He carried a laptop case by the handles with his right hand. Reaching the top of the stairs, the man saw the rows of coat hangers and the wooden shelf just above them. There were a few clothing items suspended along the stretch. He walked toward the array and removed his hat.

"You're late, you know," said a stranger, surprising the young man. The older fellow had opened the penthouse door without creating much noise.

"I am sorry, Mister . . . "

"Cedric," he flatly stated as he entered the hallway and let the apartment door close behind him. "The party. It's basically over."

"Oh, yes, that," said the man. "Long day."

"It happens," replied Cedric as he made his way to the row of coat hangers. He immediately located his long black jacket and gray scarf. "So how do you know Mr. al-Nassery?"

"Mr. al-Nassery?" he inquired with a look of confusion.

"David."

"Oh, of course."

"Long day, right?" Cedric flatly remarked.

"Exactly," he replied smiling, regaining his confidence. "We go back to the old country."

"Ah, I see," responded Cedric without suspicion as he put on his scarf and jacket. "A horrid place, as I understand—you know, with the occupation and all that."

"Yes, a horrid place, indeed. Happy to be here instead."

"Indeed. Well, David is still in there, talking to a couple of prominent folk."

"Makes sense," he responded. "After all, David never met a man he did not have a conversation with."

"Very true." Cedric laughed as he finished putting on the items. "Well, good evening."

"Good evening," replied the late visitor. Cedric seemed to pay him no further consideration as he descended the staircase. Brown jacket hanging on a hook and brown fedora resting upon the shelf, the young man readied himself. A short prayer, a few tucks and pulls at his clothes, and a breath. Gently moving his hand down the center of his own chest a few times, he took one more deep breath. From there he turned to the door, took hold of the knob, twisted it, pulled open the barrier, and entered the study.

SCENE 6

"Behold it, in all its splendor," said Cyril Williams to the host of the party. David, Williams, and Charles Harrison were in the study. The other guests had left, with the first to exit likely already at home and preparing for bed. All members of the ensemble were already gone. Only the help remained, the occasional on-the-clock person going about. George was overseeing their efforts, so David was finally able to view the printed document. His eyes scanned the three pages of text, skimming the details.

"I like it already. A marvelous work, infinite in its potentiality," said David after a few moments. "When do you plan to introduce it?"

"Next year." Williams stood beside David as the latter continued to look through the sections. "As you know, Parliament is currently on Christmas recess."

"Could you pre-file it?"

"Cyril and I do not believe that would be the finest approach," chimed in Harrison, who was standing near the wall where books filled the shelves. "We do not want people to think too much about this one. Our world is one that nitpicks much and digests little."

"Your observation is a valid one," David said, relenting. "Outside of the occasional nitpicker, who else may stand against us?"

"Well, if you mean within the House of Commons, few I can name," answered Williams. "There is Barclay. He could be a problem, given his views on the regional conflict."

"But his following is weak," interjected Harrison. "I highly doubt he will sway more than one or two members, four at the utmost."

David looked up at the two elected officials and smiled. As he did so, he heard a faint sound of the door opening but dismissed it as it corresponded with some conversation in the background between two servants. After all, his penthouse was a large dwelling that had all sorts of noises at all sorts of times.

"Charles and I will speak on behalf of it. We will introduce the bill on the very first day of the session next month. It should pass fairly quickly."

"Well then, you have made my evening yet," said the party host with a smile.

"We could always benefit from you speaking on behalf of the bill, giving a human voice to a bunch of paper."

"You know, Charles"—began Cyril as a young man softly entered the study behind him—"that sounds like a capital idea."

"Now, gentleman. I was never meant for such a stage. Who knows what cruel company may emerge as a result of my public speaking?"

"Very well, if you wish," Cyril conceded.

"So, then," said David with a breath, "I guess all I can note now is the usual, almost trite, final comments. Prepare for the worst, hope for the best—" David's words halted as he turned to face the noise of the door latching shut. His attention came to a surprise when he beheld a stoic young man standing before them. David then spoke in rising excitement at the sight of the unplanned visitor. "'And what monstrous, horrible beast slouches toward Bethlehem to be born!'"

In gleeful spirit, David rushed over to the younger man, who smiled weakly as the host embraced him. It was an awkward hug, the man turning a bit to the side as contact was made but still welcoming the hug, nonetheless. The two exchanged pleasantries before turning their attention to the two distinguished men. "Gentlemen, gentlemen, I am greatly surprised to introduce both of you to an old friend of mine—"

"Joachim." The young man shook the hands of Williams and Harrison.

"Joachim," affirmed David. "We go way back." The host looked at the new guest with intrigue. "And I must stress, I did not expect you to appear here and now."

"A friend of David's?" inquired Cyril, to which Joachim nodded in response. "Then, you are a friend of mine as well. If you need anything, let me know."

"Thank you, sir."

"Well, I—I must say," continued David. "We have a lot to recall to ourselves. I fear this has broken my train of thought on the previous matter."

"Be not concerned, David," assured Cyril. "Charles and I know what we must do. And it is so late that I dare say it is now early. Good morrow."

"Good morrow!" replied David as the two members of Parliament agreed to exit. He then directed his words to Joachim. "One moment. Let me get the other folks out." With that remark, David went off on a short search to find George and located him after a few seconds.

"George, excellent work as always with the catering and the service. An old friend just stopped by, and I'd like to start catching up. You are free to go home."

"You sure of that, Mr. al-Nassery? There's still much to be cleaned."

"Do not fret about it, kind sir. A maid service is supposed to come late afternoon on the morrow. They will see to the matter."

"Very well, Mr. al-Nassery."

"And you will get your usual rate, despite the early dismissal."

"Thank you, Mr. al-Nassery," said George, who then briefly nodded at Joachim before rounding up the rest of the help and having them leave the penthouse. With the shutting of the door, things became eerily still.

"Are we alone?" asked Joachim.

"Let me double-check the rest of the penthouse. It's a big flat, and you never quite know if a couple is not somewhere in the library necking away."

"Fair enough."

"I am fairly certain no one else is here," added David as he exited the study and entered the hallway. He shouted through the wall to George, "You can go ahead and lock the door if you prefer."

As David walked through the hallway and quickly peered into each room, Joachim turned to the closed door. With his right hand, he latched both bolts. Pulling at the knob verified that the exit was secured. He turned again to behold the study. The walls were covered with books, and two sideboards housed many bottles of wine and fine glasses. The place made him think of its owner. He thought more about what he was going to do. In a strange mental development, the tension somehow ebbed as he heard David's footsteps drawing nigh. With the opening of the door, he returned to the study with his usual smile.

"All clear, just as I presupposed."

"That is well."

David laughed. "I cannot overstate my surprise at your arrival. I really did not expect you to avoid the greatest inevitability."

"Maybe it is not the greatest inevitability, after all," rebutted Joachim with a weak smile, prompting a brief laugh from the party host.

"My, my, my, indeed," began David. "This calls for a celebration. I have my stock of good wine straight from Chaldea—a prized commodity, now that the fundamentalists took control of the place and put a stop to the industry. I save the best years for whenever former comrades show up. Would you like a drink?"

"No, thank you."

"Really?" expressed David, displaying a renewed sense of surprise. "You enjoyed it years ago. I hope the fundamentalists haven't taken control of you, also."

"Maybe they have."

David ignored the comment as went to the sideboard and took from it one of the aforementioned red wines. He placed the unopened bottle on the top of the table, where the three pages of proposed legislation were still laid out. Searching a little longer, he found a broad stem glass, one of the few not already used during the party. Placing it next to the bottle, David looked around for an opener. The investigation lasted for a few seconds while Joachim stood there, silently, seeming to be in somber spirits. After investigating the matter without success, David had a stroke of inspiration and turned to the visitor.

"Joachim, you are closer to that cupboard over there," said David as he pointed to the sideboard located to the right of his unexpected guest. "There should be a bottle opener in the top lefthand drawer. Could you please get it?"

"As a man who now has great privilege, do you still know how to use such a device?" inquired Joachim as he ventured over to the drawer and opened it.

"Try me," replied David as Joachim eyed the winged corkscrew, took hold of it, and, at David's command, tossed it underhand to the host. "It is—as the cliché goes—like riding a bicycle." David slowed his words as his concentration came upon using the device. He stabbed the cork with the screw and began to twist the top. Gradually, the wings on either side began to rise upward, as though in victory. "Once you learn how to do it, you"—David stopped twisting and then quickly pulled down both wings to pop the cork—"never forget." With a laugh of accomplishment, he tossed the cork and screw back to Joachim. The young man removed the cork from the device and then placed the opener back into the drawer while David poured himself a drink.

"I guess my faith was too small."

"Indeed." David, raised his glass to Joachim with a smile and then sipped some of the contents. "I want you to know, Joachim, that I did not forget your name. I knew it, but I was unsure if you were going under a different identity. Without clairvoyance on the matter, I just let you do the talking . . . for once."

"That is understandable, 'Mr. al-Nassery,'" said Joachim, smiling at the name.

"Well"—David laughed—"it is not a full-fledged fiction, good Joachim. As you may recall, al-Nassery was my mother's maiden name. I cannot help it that she married a British colonial officer and thus bestowed upon me the family name of Shapsdale."

"I would think that a name like Shapsdale would allow for greater upward mobility in this adopted homeland of yours."

"Come now, Joachim, the world is small. Surely, hostiles from the old country are promoting my name through assorted channels."

"Well, if not Shapsdale, then how about 'Smith,' 'Jones,' or 'Taylor'?"

"Again, Joachim, your suggestion is well-intended but ultimately logically flawed. A hundred years ago, your idea would be a strong one, a firm foundation unshaken by the winds or the rains. However, we live in a different society. This is one that values diversity, the exotic, multiculturalism and prides itself on welcoming 'the other.' Modern Western high society longs for opportunities to prove their devotion to such principles."

"And you offer them a good one," said Joachim in a dour tone. "You are the perfect balance: exotic enough to evoke interest, yet familiar enough to be considered a member of the community."

"Indeed," said David in agreement. "You can do likewise. You speak the language, understand the culture. Your name is not as infamous. You should try telling people here that your name is Joachim al-Dunya and you need assistance. Sure, many of the working-class folk may despise you; but the elites and nobles, they will love you. Especially if I offer myself as a personal reference."

"I do not plan to stay."

"Oh. Just a brief visit, then?"

"Yes," said Joachim with a sudden coldness.

David sipped his red wine, wondering at his companion's sudden change of demeanor. "Are you sure you do not want to have a drink?" he offered with a smile. "After all, 'now is the time to drink.'"

"I refuse," replied Joachim coldly. "I have found it to give me too loose of lips and too poor of thoughts. Besides, it did not help with the pain. The dread of every night, the struggle to even sleep an hour. Only now have I learned better. Only now do I know better. And after this time of darkness, I shall sleep very well."

"How will I help with that?"

Joachim al-Dunya reached into his pants pocket and pulled out a gun.

David's eyes widened when he saw the weapon revealed. It was packed in the side of Joachim's attire that David did not feel when he hugged him earlier. The handgun was a single-action semi-automatic pistol. The exterior was solid black with a dovetail sight along the barrel. It had a short recoil and a ten-round capacity magazine.

Al-Dunya had cocked back the hammer as soon as he pointed it at Shapsdale, aiming it at his chest.

"And so it is," stoically replied David, who brimmed with existential terror. He looked into his old friend's emotionless eyes. He knew he had no means of escape, and no one was near enough to rescue him. They were alone, with the only exit locked and located behind Joachim. His composure remained firm, as this was not the first time that someone had pointed a firearm at him. However, he became openly perplexed as Joachim did not take the next logical action. "Is this the greatest inevitability? Does death equate to a permanent pause to the moment of transport? Or is it that time itself has slowed, and moments now equal minutes? No, not that. It is you, Joachim, who has halted."

Joachim remained silent.

"So what is it that leads to this delay, O beloved assassin? Is it nerves, the fear of terminating a human life? No, not that. I know you very well. You are not one to shy away from such an act. Truly, your weapon does not even shake. Perchance, you seek funds, and this is a robbery? Not likely. Your face is not covered, nor are your hands gloved. You knew I would recognize you, making this a very flawed attempt at stealth. So what is it? End my speculative ramblings and tell me the story."

"You will die this evening," stated Joachim. "Just not yet."

"That's a relief," David lightly noted, though he remained shaken.

"This will not be a mere blood vengeance. I have not come here solely to shoot you and then run like some criminal. Tonight will not be a night of mere bloodletting, a primitive act for a savage monster. No, David Shapsdale. Tonight will be so much more. Before the trigger is pulled, before the deed is done, we shall see your past. We will return to the old country, to why this night has come to be."

"That sounds respectable, enough," spoke David. "So where do we start?"

"It is late. I shall take a seat, as will you," stated Joachim, who sat down at the nearest chair and, with the pointing of his handgun, beckoned David to do likewise. They sat at two chairs facing opposite each other by the small table that did not have the bill laid out upon it. Joachim carefully placed the gun onto the top of the table and then, with the tips of his fingers, turned the device so that the barrel faced Shapsdale. "It was good to finally sit down, for I have survived quite the journey."

"Indeed," said David, wine glass still in hand. "So have I."

ACT II

Scene 1

The desert. A seemingly vacant space. An empty realm, lacking vegetation, grand cities, and water. Sweltering during the day and chilling during the night. This intrinsically hostile setting was nevertheless pockmarked by oases and towns, villages and kind strangers, roaming tribes, and occasional modern technology. Some areas had paved roads serving as highways, with few traffic lights or stop signs to halt the velocity of passing vehicles. Wildlife of varying kinds inhabited the region. Nothing as physically impressive as the beasts in more fertile regions, but many species, nonetheless.

It was a region of historical violence. For millennia, armies fought each other for control of this vast sea of sand. Tribes raided tribes; Old Testament kings battled; empires stretched their arms into the pool of barren terrain; and eager conquerors of classical powers made their reputation and, sometimes, lost their lives. Conflict after conflict beset the region, which was positioned between so many different civilizations. So many wars befell the area that some considered it a miracle that the sand was not a reddish tint, attesting to all of the blood absorbed by its surface over the ages.

In keeping with the law of superposition, vestiges of the most recent military venture were situated on the surface of the dunes.

One point of particular interest was an abandoned tank. A machine of impressive power and daunting noise, it once carried along the field with the rolling tracks along its wheels. It had climbed over the dusty heights, crushing enemies and overtaking entrenchments. Its gun pounded the ramparts of the foe to dust, blasting away all security. It sped through the badlands, gulping its precious oil as its sweaty inhabitants dried their brows in the search for the next antagonist.

And yet, no more for that one tank. No historian knew its particular demise. Whatever the cause, it was not a peaceful end. Along its port side was a gaping hole, large enough for a man to climb into and out of. The frame crumpled but mostly held together, for the projectile had its fullest fury emptied into the frail bodies of the crew. As years had passed, vandals stole pieces of the wreck, some for souvenirs and others for raw materials. Rust was wearing away the armor plates, while the remains of the crew were scattered bones in shredded clothing. Winds carried sheets of sand that covered the interior flooring and submerged much of its track, which was missing many wheels, thanks to scavengers.

The tank stood vigil in homage to the old war. Other vehicles and men were destroyed during that battle. Other ruined machines smoldered in defeat. However, they were removed; either refitted or sold for scrap. Corpses were buried in mass graves. Only that one machine remained, presented by itself as an informal monument to the disastrous campaign, a rotting reminder of who lost the conflict. The destroyed structure was a heavy sight for the minds residing within the nearby village. That village had offered their support to the losing side. It was common to see folks in mourning by that old gutted tank, especially on the anniversaries of the war's end.

David Shapsdale stood next to it. He was alive and conscious for the war, though too tender an age to serve. His diverse background prompted neutrality among his parents, but all his friends and their families were of one mind on the matter. The rotting tank reminded him of those foolish days, when the two armies fought, and when the side his friends and he adored was vanquished. He cried and prayed with them as the news of loved ones killed in action became commonplace. Then, the truly tragic announcement. The battles were halted, the territory lost; and the occupation began.

David was not near the ruined machine that afternoon to remember sadder times. There had been times when he visited it alone in contemplation, yet he was focused now on the quick instead of the dead, the moving rather than the immobile. In disdain, he beheld the paved road, its dark asphalt appearing all the darker because of the contrast with the faded gold sands. There was a minor procession at hand, a series of tan military vehicles. A few of them were tanks, models that were more advanced than the shell beside David. They had better armor and more guns, the main weapon packing greater power than a generation ago. Jeeps were also in the line, carrying various personnel and supplies. There were a couple of large trucks bearing troops with rifles and body armor. He counted twenty-three automobiles in all, which was typical for a patrol in that area.

"I prefer them all dead, buried over the noise of taps and wailing widows," proclaimed a voice behind him. The declaration shook David from his thoughts, causing him to turn around and behold a familiar face—a man around his age with a welcoming face that he had worked alongside at a local shop for years.

"Hello, Kadmon." David nodded, lifting his voice to compensate for the loud droning of the nearby convoy. "Come to see the show, huh?"

"No, David," he replied, walking through the sifting sand to get closer. "I came to invite you to something."

"A party?"

"You could say that," Kadmon commented.

"And what do you say?"

"You know how much we hate those soldiers marching around our homeland? How we complain about it a lot? And how we wished somebody would step up and do something?"

"A joyful, leisurely activity, to be sure."

"Well, I just got word that old Moab is holding a meeting at his place."

"The rich fellow you started working for a few months ago?"

"That would be him," said Kadmon, nodding. "He wants me to bring at least one person to the party. And you seem like the perfect kind of man to bring in."

"When does this party happen?"

Kadmon hesitated before replying. "In about an hour."

"A little last minute, you think?" said David, who became cynical. "You asked a bunch of other people before me, didn't you?"

"Well . . . I . . . um . . . yes, I did."

"And none of them said yes?"

Kadmon answered with silence.

"Shame, Kadmon, shame."

"Hey, I was going to bring you into it eventually. It's just that, you know, you are not entirely one of us, if you catch my drift."

David folded his arms and remained silent.

"Do you want to come or not?"

"Do I want to associate with a higher caste, dwell inside a bountiful little palace? And maybe get to complain about our sad political affairs? Sounds good to me."

Kadmon and David walked back to the village and from there to the villa. An impressive facility, it looked like a military compound with its high surrounding wall, cameras, and a small staff of armed security. There were some small children running around and a few attractive young women watching over the little creatures. The two young men made their way to the proper meeting room, the guards nodding as the duo walked by. Soon, they were inside an elegant, yet clandestine, chamber.

"Make yourself comfortable," said Kadmon. "Our gracious host will be here shortly."

"Thank you." David nodded as Kadmon exited. A couple minutes later, another man entered the room, coming in from a different door. He smiled when he saw David and approached him with a hearty handshake.

"Hello there, neighbor."

"Greetings," said David as he shook his hand. There was a certain familiarity to the fellow, though David was unable to quite place it. He was shorter than Shapsdale and had a hungry sparkle to his eyes.

"You seem puzzled, neighbor."

"I guess it is just that"—David hesitated—"I was brought in here merely a few minutes ago, and I do not believe I know the fullest extent of what I have agreed to."

"Do not fret, my new friend. If Kadmon has sent you here, it is for the right reasons," he said. "He told me to come here if I was interested in solving the problem of our race."

"Yes, those lousy soldiers. You would think for all their cries of sympathy our brethren abroad would come to our aid."

"They are afraid to. Oh yes, they will build up their armies, place some regiments on the borders—but that will be all."

"I am sorry"—conceded David—"but I cannot help but feel that I have met you somewhere. Your body is alien to my eyes, but your voice is so familiar to my ears."

"I think I know your situation," said the man, flaunting himself in pride. "Maybe it would help if you knew that my name is Girgash Keniz."

"Of course!" exclaimed David as his eyes widened. "That is it. The Girgash Keniz of radio fame. Your denunciations of the occupation have long filled my leisure."

"Well," said Keniz in feigned bashfulness, "always a joy to meet a fan."

Their conversation was ended when four people entered the room. Kadmon was the lead figure, smiling at Girgash and David. Behind him was a pretty, modestly attired woman, who carried a serving dish balancing a wine bottle and four glasses. There was also another man, about the same age and appearance as Kadmon. He looked less joyful and carried a more professional expression. At the center of the four people was the man behind the occasion. Heavyset and limping, he used a cane that had a black stem topped with an ivory bulb. His formal suit was specifically measured and sewn for his body. With salt-and-pepper hair and wrinkled skin, he was the most elderly of those in the room. He was also the richest, given that he owned the villa.

"Gentlemen," began Kadmon, "let me introduce you to Moab, our gracious and patriotic host." Kadmon then directed his attention to the old man, who had stopped walking and was standing with cane to the side. "Moab, you told me to bring someone, and I brought two! Girgash Keniz and David Shapsdale."

"Good evening, gentlemen," stated Moab, reservedly.

"A pleasure to meet you, kind sir," said David as he approached him and shook hands. Girgash followed after.

"And this is Perziz Repha, a fellow employee of Moab," explained Kadmon, gesturing to the other man. "He was the one who told me about this little meeting." Again, hands were shaken and verbal introductions made. "If Moab so permits, we can all sit down now."

The elder man nodded and all, save the servant woman, took a seat.

"As I was explaining, Moab, these men will help us with the cause. Girgash's qualities you already know, but David's might not be as revealed."

"Why are you here?" inquired Moab of David. His tone was not threatening.

"I hate being occupied."

"I see," said Moab, giving a slight smile. "Then you have arrived at the most correct of locations, for we are here to end that occupation and make a new independent country." Moab paused to examine David. "Do you have any particularly bad memories of the old war?"

"Well," David pondered, "not really. I was a child when it ended. Bad things happened to some of my friends, their families."

"I see," said Moab, shifting deeper into his plush chair. "I have plenty of memories of the battles and the wars. Tanks would roam my village's roads, paving them with tracks. If you were not careful, then you could be gravely injured."

"Is that why you have a limp?"

"He is a smart man, this David," said Moab to Kadmon, before redirecting his attention to Shapsdale. "Yes, a tank did this and more. My brother—he was older—was sniped off when he got too close. He was only trying to help me. In that respect, having avoided the greatest inevitability of man, I can say that my situation is not as horrible. I merely have to make sure that I do not run, skip, jump, or stand unsupported for too long; and I'll be fine."

"Yours is a victim status shared by the whole of this land," declared Girgash.

"Indeed," replied Moab, whose tone became lighter. "Shall we drink?"

"Already that hour?" questioned Girgash.

"Yes, the sun does make its motion so gallantly. In its course in the sky, I can say that the time is such that drinks are in order," said David.

"Then, we drink," stated Moab. He snapped his fingers and the female servant went about the room, distributing wine glasses. The bottle was already opened. She poured contents into each glass, getting a short statement of thanks from David only. "I have come quite accustomed to this life, and I think I deserve it."

"Sounds like the old divine right," David said, critically.

"Maybe, I don't know," responded Moab. "Regardless, it is not my intention to do any true fighting. I am past that possibility. If you want to, you can. However, you can understand why I will not be joining you as you both travel with Perziz to Chaldea."

"Chaldea?" David nearly choked in surprise while drinking his fermented potable. "That miserable town?"

"I am equally surprised." Girgash spoke up. "There is not much there to boast about."

"Its backwardness, if one may, shall be the perfect point of boasting. Chaldea will be our centerpiece, our capital for the time being. That is, until the preferred city is divulged by the enemy. Who knows? Maybe we will be so satisfied with the rustic environment that it will become our new capital."

"But Moab, my host, I wonder about such a decision. After all, has anything good ever come out of Chaldea?" asked David.

"The very wine you enjoy, Mr. Shapsdale, was from that place. For all its backwardness, their vineyards are the unsung heroes of high society. I would put their beloved contents against any challenger from Italy or France."

"It is also a good place for it lacks a military presence," added Kadmon. "It is a pure society, devoid of such a despicable species."

"The two of you should be very useful. Girgash, a popular voice of dissent so blameless that he was shut down by the military," said Moab. "And David . . . Kadmon told me simply that you were a man up to the challenge."

"I hope so, Moab."

"I shall send with you Perziz Repha, a long-time friend of mine who will serve as an intermediary between us. This warning I give you: this will be a cruel operation."

"I am ready," stated a determined David. "No matter the act, no matter the effort. For us, for our cause."

Moab smiled at the younger man. He raised his glass in a tacit toast. Kadmon and Perziz did likewise. Finally, David joined them, giving a sinister smile that was amplified with the raising of his glass.

SCENE 2

Around the time that David Shapsdale was meeting with Moab and the others, another meeting was about to take place. Eighty miles away from the villa, the roads were paved, with plenty of traffic lights and signs. Every edifice had electricity that worked all hours and clean, running water. Most of the folks were college-educated and had ready access to doctors, lawyers, elected officials, reporters, and grocery stores. There, many languages were spoken, and many ethnicities were represented. A culturally diverse environment where the cosmopolitan and the traditional somehow coexisted.

In that particular building, it was the military that reigned. Armed service was mandatory for most citizens; however, only a minority went beyond the required minimal of three years. Some, however, sought a career in the uniformed forces.

She was seated in the waiting room. She was a little nervous, mostly because of the stories she was told about her new superior. Fresh out of college and basic training, her time between arrival and the meeting was spent looking over the paperwork meant for the officer. Like most people in that room, seated or walking about, she wore an olive green uniform with black shoes and a black beret. Her hair, which was also black, was shoulder-length and tied into a ponytail. Having reviewed the papers yet again, she placed them back into the folder.

Taking a breath, she leaned back into her seat. In the corner there was a box TV set. It was tuned to a local news station and put on low volume. Its screen was average size. The receptionist wanted to get a larger set for that corner area, but anything bigger would have been too thick to place on the small table. Still, it was a newer model, with its biggest technological achievement being the lack of rabbit ears. Magazines were stacked on another small table, placed at another corner of the square room. She was thinking about grabbing one of the periodicals to pass the time when the woman at the front desk, one of the few civilians employed at the facility, spoke up.

"Private Shiri Dahan?"

"Yes?" she asked as she rose from her chair.

"Corporal Greenberg should be ready for you shortly. You can go ahead into her office," said the receptionist.

"Okay, thank you," said Shiri, who smiled as she walked past the front desk with the folder held under her left arm.

The activity of going from the waiting room to the hallway helped a little bit with the nerves. After walking past the front desk and then past a couple of other privates who were headed outside, she stopped before a black marquee sign hung on the wall. White letters explained in detail where each office was for each important person. A quick study of the information led her to find the room number for Greenberg. With a nod and a smile, she went down the hall until she found the office.

Her mild angst returned as she neared the office. Its door was ajar, and she could hear shouting. Given the occasional pause and lack of audible response, she concluded that the argument must have been over the phone. She halted before the entrance, the forceful declarations on the other side making her wonder about the ease of her assignment. Nevertheless, this was not optional and she knew it. Composing herself and double-checking the properness of her uniform, she pushed the door open and entered.

"Yes, I know that there was a treaty," a visibly annoyed Greenberg spoke into the receiver of her landline phone. "I don't care... Why don't I care? Because they don't care!" Dahan stood at attention with the folder under her arm. Her superior looked up briefly, quickly glancing the new arrival and then returning to her agitated conversation. "If you think you saw something, get a better look. This is not hard . . . What happens if we go into the borderlands . . . You should be asking what happens if that turns out to be a group of hostiles . . . Get a better look and call me back. If it is something bad, then I will be there . . . And yes, yes, I will take all responsibility. I always do . . . Shalom." Slamming the receiver, the officer immediately turned her attention to the newcomer. "Yes?"

"Private Shiri Dahan reporting for duty, ma'am," she said with a salute and a faint smile.

Her superior looked at her with cold blue eyes, neither delving into anger nor welcome. Greenberg briefly saluted back.

"I have my orders and my papers right here."

Her superior beckoned her to approach. Dahan placed the folder on Greenberg's desk. Her superior opened it. There were various items of note, including a college transcript, a one-page curriculum vitae, and a few letters from high command. Shiri remained standing, fidgeting a little in her place. In past meetings, she did not recall the reviews of her paperwork being as thorough. Sometimes, no review was taken.

To pass what felt like a long time, Shiri looked at the person and the place before her. Corporal Greenberg was a stern-looking creature. In addition to the blue eyes and pinkish skin, she contrasted with Shiri on hair color also. While partially obscured by a beret, Greenberg had a brownish-blonde head of hair. She later learned that her superior was also taller by several inches, striking an imposing five feet ten inches without boots, which she often wore and thus presented an even more towering figure. Her face and neck had deep lines, created by the twin forces of her age and the stress of her position.

Her office was full of things, all of which appeared work-related. No family photos and few books. Instead, she had several shelves of VHS tapes. Each one had a light strip of masking tape placed along the spine with notes describing its contents. There were a few piles of cassettes as well, mostly recordings from interrogations and recent phone taps. There were no copies of casual listening music. She had two wooden desks, one larger than the other, and placed in an L-shape. The longer one was closest to the entrance and had several papers on it, even before the folder was given. The shorter one had a computer with a beige body and a thick monitor. There was a mouse on one side of the screen and a short stack of floppy disks on the other. As she saw these things, Shiri wondered why it is was taking so long for Greenberg to sift through the folder of papers.

"First assignment?" asked Corporal Ruth Greenberg. The utterance returned Shiri's attention back to her new superior, who said this without looking up from the paperwork.

"Since basic training, yes."

"So, you have never experienced any shots fired in anger."

"Correct."

"Take a seat," stated Greenberg.

Shiri smiled fleetingly as she saw that there was no chair in front of the desk. Two were along the wall to her left. She grabbed one of them, placed it in front of the desk, and then sat down. Upon sitting down, she waited for more conversation. Dahan placed her hands on her lap, one gripping the other to stop them from shaking. So far, what others had said was true.

Shuffling the papers back in order, Greenberg stuffed them into the folder, closed it, and then pushed it to the side before raising her eyes to look at the smiling subordinate. "All seems to be in order."

Shiri breathed in relief.

"Is there some reason why you are smiling right now?"

"Umm, well." Shiri hesitated. "It is a tendency, Corporal Greenberg. Regardless, if you want me to stop, I will take all necessary measures to do so."

"As long it does not interfere with your work, that should not be necessary."

"Thank you, Corporal."

"I saw that General Moshe signed your papers."

"Yes, the general did."

"Daniel and I go back some years. Are you well-acquainted with him?"

"He and my father are good friends. Our families live in the same neighborhood."

"Terrific," spoke Greenberg sarcastically, evidently drawing her own conclusions. "What did Moshe and his friends tell you about me?"

"Permission to speak freely?"

"Yes, go ahead."

"Well," began Shiri, carefully thinking through her statements. "Well, um, they said that you are committed; you were passionate, courageous, smart—"

"Quit sucking up," interjected Ruth, removing Shiri's smile. "I want to know what else they said about me."

"Well, they, um, they—after they said all those nice things, they warned me that you can be a little, how do I put it . . . "

"Just use their exact words, private."

"Okay. They said you were a little paranoid," replied Shiri, building her courage as she went along. "They said that while you are competent, you seem desperate for a fight and eager to assume the worst of every situation. One of General Moshe's friends went as far as to say he was afraid you would start the next war."

"Do you agree with them?" asked Greenberg, staring at Shiri. The glare was discomforting.

"Permission to speak—"

"Yes. I want to know."

"Well, Corporal . . . I mean, I'm not one for politics, but I keep track of things. There hasn't been a war in nearly twenty years. There are treaties in place; and, and of course, the boycott was lifted. So— truth be told—I find their statements, literally, reasonable."

Shiri wondered what was going to happen next. The silence felt very long.

Greenberg removed the stare and looked back down at the desktop. "Understand this, Private Dahan: the war is not over." Greenberg then returned to staring at the young woman in front of her. "Yes, there may be treaties; there may be an overall absence of violence; but the war continues. We do not have peace now; we only have an absence of war. And never, ever, mistake the two."

"Yes, corporal."

"The mentality that gave birth to the violence decades back—the unbridled hatred for people like you and me—that mentality still exists. It is on the edges now; but at any point, it can reemerge. As my father always says, 'Just because there's a God in Heaven, doesn't mean there isn't a devil in Hell.'"

"Yes, corporal."

"Anyway," said Greenberg, shifting her tone from determined to professional, "your space should be ready in a couple of days. You'll have a desk and your own computer situated in this room. Do not expect too much chatter during the work hours. And do not waste your time on the social media sites."

"What is social media?" innocently inquired Shiri.

"Not sure, myself. It's a new name I heard from some young techies on the second floor. That's what they keep calling a new set of websites that just got launched. Something about being able to talk with people and share photos and stuff."

"I thought that was what email was for."

"Either way, I do not want to catch you spending time on those sites when you are on the clock. Is that understood?"

"Yes, corporal."

Then, the phone rang, ending the in-person conversation. Greenberg noted which line was attempting communication. She pushed the blinking button and then picked up the receiver, its coiled wire stretching toward her. "Well, do you have an update . . . Okay . . . Okay . . . " Greenberg's facial expression changed. "And you are sure . . .

Okay, then. I will be there in fifteen minutes. Shalom." Greenberg slammed down the receiver and got up, quickly gathering her things. "You just got your first mission. There is a confirmed report of suspicious movement along the border. A guard just confirmed that at least one person is armed. And we will be there."

"Yes, corporal," responded Shiri as her superior quickly dashed out of the office, prompting her newly assigned subordinate to chase after her.

SCENE 3

Sand dominated the frontier. It covered centuries of history, it hid countless little creatures with stingers and claws. The winds were pushing it along the region, beating it against the three men journeying toward Chaldea. Nothing too drastic. The gusts were weak, never rising the tide of shiny grains beyond the kneecaps. The stingers and the claws did not strike, either. Despite the tender mercies allotted, the venture was still a tough one for those who had to walk. A beating sun, hot air, heavy backpacks, and rugged ground led to a stressful trip from that comfortable villa to the jerkwater town.

"None of us live south of the poverty line, and yet still we have to do this by foot," lamented Perziz Repha, who was at the front and knew how to get to Chaldea.

"Spoiled fellow, are you not?" asked Girgash Keniz, walking alongside David Shapsdale.

"Merely a man who realizes that he should not have to do certain things. This whole time of my life shall be proof if you ask me," replied Perziz.

"I wasn't."

"Nor was I," said David as he wiped the sweat off his forehead. "Remind me, where is everyone else?"

"They are back about twenty miles or so, resting comfortably in a climate-controlled mansion," responded Girgash.

"Sipping and, or gulping the precious fine wines, no doubt," replied David, whose tone became theatrical to the visible amusement of Girgash. "They drink, drink, and drink some more, wasting away in their heavy, encompassing couches and chairs, resting and adding diameter to their bellies. They get sicker and sicker every week, fattened for the slaughter of death to come, ruing as they lay yet again, but this time on a bed, 'Nothing! Nothing! We did nothing with our wretched lives!'"

"You're a regular jester, you know that?" noted Perziz in an irritated tone.

"Humor gets me through the eternal annoyance of class found here, as the wealthiest and most domesticated lay lazily so in their castles far from our location, while we head toward a destination doomed to misery," replied David as they began ascending a dune.

"Misery? You are a pessimist, I fear."

"Now, I am many things, Girgash, but not that," retorted David. "I am only a pessimist when the glass is half-empty. Whenever the glass is half-full, I am an optimist."

Going up the dune took them to a promising sight. While they slapped the sand off their clothing as best they could, they beheld their destination in the distance. It was hard to capture details, but the three were able to see the distant features of several minarets and a couple of onion domes. Some of the land ahead was fertile, irrigated into an artificial oasis. A few wells also helped bring civilization to that desolate place. The three men stopped to take hold of the nearing end of their journey.

"Chaldea," stated Perziz.

"Duly noted," said David, again wiping his forehead.

"Did we have to walk all the way there?" lamented Girgash, who dried his sweaty face and neck with his sleeve.

"If we came with the garments of kings, the soldiers would arrive ready as though expecting kings. We come as peasants; they know not where or when we come," Perziz replied, seeming to ignore his own past complaints.

"Point taken." David sighed. "And then, your glorious struggle."

"*Our* glorious struggle," corrected Girgash. "Don't forget that we are all in this fight."

"A fight that we lost some time ago, unless I have erred in my historical knowledge."

"Then why are you here?" asked Perziz.

"Just to get you angry," David said, smiling.

"I would hold your tongue, David. Save your cruelties for the enemy," stated Girgash, playing the peacemaker. "This trip has taken its toll on us all. Perziz, is there a prepared place for sleep and food?"

"An inn, which has reserved beds for two of us," stated Perziz, eliciting confused looks from his weary co-journeymen. He then pulled out a gun. "I guess I was not very honest with either of you. Out of the desert shall come two men, not three."

"A cruel fate for the third man, yes?" calmly quipped David. By contrast, Girgash responded with outrage, directing his anger at Perziz.

"We walked through the threshing sands together, with blowing winds and hostile nights only to have you murder one of us?"

"One of you two will murder the other," ordered Perziz, his gun pointed at both Girgash and David. "Do it out here, where the sands and vultures can remove the corpse."

"What would we kill each other with?" continued an angry Girgash, offering any and all possible arguments. "Nothing but sand all around us, not even a good-sized boulder or cinder to dash upon the head of the victim."

"You will have to make the decision, Perziz," said David.

"You will fight to the death," reiterated Perziz. "I don't care how you two resort to figuring out who will be the man to sleep in a nice bedroom and who will be the one who does not wake up."

"Are you not listening to Girgash? There is nothing here for us to use! Only that precious gun of yours is worth its weight to kill," said David.

"When I say so, the two of you shall fight; and the winner will have to kill his opponent with his bare hands," continued Perziz.

"But there is no reason to," insisted Girgash. "We all believe in the same cause." His words, however, only seemed to cause Perziz to remain convicted.

"Because Moab, the mastermind of our operations, knows that only two of us shall be allowed to enter Chaldea," said Perziz. "I am a childhood friend of his; he came to my father's house when his brother was killed. Because he cried in my arms, we are brothers. He told me the plan, and I now tell you: fight to the death. I don't care who wins."

"You are insane, Perziz. This would only make us weaker. Our enemies do not enact such killings in their ranks, so why should we do it?" David critically asked, his voice rising.

"Perziz, what if David and I decided that *you* were the one who was not going to make it out of the desert?" asked Girgash. "You can't kill us both and return to your Moab with the knowledge that all the recruits taken in one day are dead. I doubt even he will approve of such conduct."

"Loyalty rests solely in our race. If you cannot kill for your race, for your country, then you are not worthy."

"This is gratuitous, and I demand that you hand over that gun of yours," declared David, getting a nod of support from Girgash.

"Fight to the death," insisted Perziz, though in a weaker tone.

"Perziz!" shouted David. "If you don't hand that gun to me, I will simply walk away; and Girgash, my friend, shall walk with me."

"I said—"

"Nothing of value to me," interrupted a driven David. "Hand the gun over. I have money of my own, and I will gladly pay for another room."

"The orders were to have—"

"None of this foolishness," interjected David, whose words were evidently getting to the mentality of Perziz. His aim was lowering, the handgun's muzzle facing the sand. "Girgash, myself, and you—yes, even you—will go to Chaldea without problem. I will even play the gentleman and let you two sleep inside, and I'll sleep under the stars."

"The fight—"

"Doesn't have to take place," said David. "Just give me the gun, and you'll feel a lot better. I promise I won't kill you."

Perziz began to think. His words had ceased. There was silence between the three men. Girgash looked back and forth between David and Perziz. David stared at the man with the firearm. Perziz kept his glance to the ground, his grip of the gun loosening. After several moments of discernment, Perziz looked up at David and walked a few steps toward him. Then, he sighed.

"Here, then. Take it," said a defeated Perziz to David.

The voice of reason smiled and approached Perziz, whose hand was outstretched and held the gun on the top of his hand rather than gripping the trigger. David took hold of the weapon.

"Thank you, David," said Girgash in breathed relief amid the lowered tension. "It's good to know you're a soldier of sanity. For I doubt that I could ever kill anyone, let alone you."

David then shot Girgash in the chest. He did so in a casual manner, turning to face his acquaintance, raising his arm, and pulling the trigger. The act was committed without hesitation.

A stunned Girgash hobbled a few steps, looking at David and then at the gaping wound that painted his chest red. He looked momentarily at his killer before falling backward into the dune, landing into a pool of sand that partially submerged his corpse. David turned to Perziz, whose shocked expression mirrored Girgash's.

"As I was saying, I won't kill you," spoke David in a calm voice, handing the firearm back to Perziz. "On to Chaldea, then?"

"Yes, David," replied an evidently impressed Perziz. "On to Chaldea."

Scene 4

"'There may be times when we are powerless to prevent injustice, but there must never be a time when we fail to protest,'" quoted David, seated in his study after the evening party. He was looking at his wine glass. There were only a few small drops remaining, coalesced at the very bottom of the bowl.

"Elie Wiesel," flatly replied Joachim al-Dunya, who was sitting nearest to the pistol, its muzzle still aimed at the owner of the penthouse, even though the trigger was not gripped by either man.

"His words seemed relevant at this hour, reminiscing and all that."

"You talk of the cause again, as though it still had some foothold in the mountain of benevolence," observed Joachim.

"It did, and it does," insisted David, focusing on the empty glass. He held the goblet tenderly, as though it were his child.

"The next thing you will tell me," replied Joachim with mild anger, "some like-minded universality. Absolute relevance and acceptance, the great cause that you so wanted. The eternal justice so desired by the underdog, for some injustice somewhere is an injustice everywhere."

"Yes, my next quote to state in my arguments. The words of other people make more sense, which is why I use them so liberally," said David.

"Misquoted," countered Joachim. "You misquoted so many."

"That is a matter of opinion."

"Through the desert, even then a heartless murderer."

"Murderer?" exclaimed David in feigned surprise, turning his attention from the empty glass to his unexpected company. "Not me. I am a harmless old man, whose times are spent chasing young men's dreams. I am not the type for it."

"But the voice of our people, Girgash Keniz. You shot him dead in blood as frigid as any winter."

"That was survival."

"You had the gun; you could have let everyone live. It was a gun not unlike this one," said Joachim, examining the piece on the table and caressing its frame. "Life was never that precious to you, was it?"

"No man is ever happy to learn that he is a second-class citizen."

"Was human life so petty that you spilled it even when it was unnecessary?"

"No people should be treated as we were treated. Not even those pig-bloods," stated David, giving extra disgust when uttering that last pejorative phrase.

"Still clinging to absurdities?"

"I would doubt that," said David, who looked down at the glass again and its dregs. "Can I, at least, get up to get another drink? As of late I get easily parched without it."

"If you must."

David smiled and pushed back his chair. Rising up, he walked back to the other table, where the latest bottle to be opened on that festive evening remained alone and on top of the legislative bill. Leaning the bottle over so that the crimson contents poured into the broad bowl, he carefully set the container down and took hold of the glass by the stem.

"Is it the only way you can get a good night's sleep?" Joachim interrupted as David took another drink.

"Merely remembering the cause is sufficient," David stated in defense, proceeding to take a swig of the newly filled glass.

"You still believe we were right."

"Yes, I do," replied David as he remained standing at the small table with the bottle and bill copy. "We wanted our independence. Name a race that doesn't."

"That justified coming to that one hole in the desert and calling it home? Turning that isolated bastion of sanity into a center of fire?"

David took another drink and then walked back to his seat opposite Joachim. "It was a bastion of sanity. And we spread that sanity to the ends of the world and back."

"If what you call sanity was the thing that spread, then I have truly underestimated your indifference to suffering."

"You still have the peach fuzz of a man your age. We did not spread suffering; we spread hope amongst our people."

Joachim took an especial offense to being labeled young. He held this emotion within, however. He was controlled; he was conditioned. So he calmly put forth his objection to David's remarks as the party host sat down. "I have seen as much as you, David. I have reached and surpassed your age even if my mother came and delivered me into this vapor of a life after you. Your hair grays, mine grows. But we are very much, by measure of experience, the same age. A great mountain that is eroding, a small mountain that is jutting upward. When one falls to medium height and the other rises to medium height, to the climber they are identical. They are brothers in scope, whose disparity is invisible."

"Just wait until the others hear about tonight," opined David in a lighthearted way, evidently attempting to cut down the serious tone of his company.

Joachim looked down and smirked briefly. His expression when facing David again mirrored the latter's former confidence.

"There are no more others."

It was genuine surprise to David, who had made no effort to keep track of the fates of his former associates. He was a man who seldom went online and never reached out on social media. They fled—as he had—several years earlier. He wondered if his younger peer was lying, but the sincerity of his condition led him to conclude otherwise. In an evening where his best soldier had become his greatest foe, nothing seemed impossible. In silence, he took another drink from his newly filled glass. Then, he raised it up in partial reverence, toasting those who had fallen since the flight from the old country.

"I guess it was your handiwork," David posited.

"In a manner of speaking."

"And so, they have experienced the greatest inevitability."

"Indeed, but not the one you assume," replied Joachim, garnering a somewhat confused expression from the penthouse apartment owner.

SCENE 5

Perziz Repha and David Shapsdale received scant notice when they entered Chaldea. The community was not as backward as they presupposed. Most streets had a basic layer of asphalt and others even bore markings. There were several automobiles, and the three biggest intersections had a four-way traffic light suspended by cables. Nearly every building had antennae of varying sizes and designs perched atop their ceilings, aiding in the reception of television channels and sluggish internet. The modern conveniences contrasted with outdoor shops, untreated water, and a low standard of living; the best domiciles and apartments came only to those whose whole families, including children, labored long hours in various manufacturing capacities. There were still plenty who were affected by the recent downturn in the economy and lacked much of anything.

The majority of the people worked for the wine industry. Nearly all of Chaldea's border with the barren world was marked with vegetation. Grapes were grown by the legion, then gathered and fermented. Despite the town being overwhelmingly Muslim, plenty of folk worked in the process. Most rationalized that their activities did not involve the actual creation of wine but rather simply the growing and picking of grapes or merely the packaging and transporting of goods. Those specifically involved in the most haram stage of the practice was a small group of Christians and secular Persian immigrants who lacked a religious or moral objection to creating potent drinkables.

Repha and Shapsdale entered onto main street, a place dominated by slow-moving vehicles and ample amounts of pedestrians. Dozens of small businesses and shops—some in brick-and-mortar facilities, others under temporary tents—lined the area. The shouts of merchants and customers haggling went on uninfluenced by the new arrivals, neither of whom made eye contact with the barterers. After walking a couple more blocks, Perziz halted; and David did the same, as the latter knew not the location of the inn. Perziz removed his backpack and placed it on the ground. Also bearing a heavy load, David was only too happy to do the same as his traveling companion.

"Stay here with the luggage," ordered Perziz. "The hotel is only a few blocks away, but I want to double check that it is safe."

"You think Girgash is following us from the grave?"

"I should be back in a few minutes. While I am gone . . . well, just don't be irresponsible," firmly stated Perziz, who then turned away and walked down the street, seeming to be cautious.

"Just don't be irresponsible," said David to himself, mocking Perziz. "I probably shot the wrong man, after all." He laughed aloud at the thought.

His laughter abruptly terminated when he felt the rushing crash of a human body slam into him. The impact nearly caused him to fall, though he had enough balance to maintain his footing. The source of the blow was from his side, away from his pondering gaze into the streets' activity. David turned his head to see the origin of the tackle. He saw on the ground a young man with messy hair, panting heavily. He was scrawny and his clothes were worn. Wide-eyed, the boy stumbled back to a standing position and approached David in fear and trembling. He gripped a wallet in one hand.

"Sorry, sorry, sir," he exclaimed over and over. "I'm really, really sorry, sir. Please, please don't turn me over. Please, don't!"

David was amused by his desperation. "Not my intention, young lad," he assured him, the rest of the people around apathetic to the drama. "Now, tell me, where are they coming from?"

"That lousy 'friend' I called him," stated the youth between breaths. "He left me high and dry. I should have . . . I should have . . . I . . . I don't know."

"Poor of speech, empty of stomach, I presume," observed David. "Run down that street and I'll tell them you went a different way."

"Thank you, thank you so very much!"

"But," stressed David, "I expect you to meet me here, at that hookah bar over there specifically, tomorrow morn."

"Morning?" asked the visibly confused young man, who seemed more boy than adult.

"Yes, morning," politely explained David. "What is your name?"

"Joachim," the youth stated after some hesitation.

"Do you understand where to meet me, Joachim?" asked David.

"Yes, yes, yes, I do. Thank you!" exclaimed Joachim as he bumbled past David and then reached a fast speed to disappear into the crowded byway.

"No, *thank you*," stated David.

Seconds later, a pair of authorities jogged up the street. Angrily looking around the area, they began to ask about a young pickpocket seen fleeing from a crime scene. While others could not recall or gave uncertain testimony, David volunteered information. His confidence won the trust of the two law enforcers, who took his word and went the opposite direction of the desperate young man that David had encountered moments earlier.

"David," said a returning Perziz, returning to his travel companion four minutes after the police exited on their futile hunt.

"Yes?"

"The inn is safe. Let's go," ordered Perziz, who stooped to pick up his backpack and put the heavy item on. David did likewise, and the two soon left the street corner and were off to the motel.

Just as they exited, the young man that collided with David returned to the scene. Exhausted and breathing hard, legs and lungs being sore, he collapsed upon a bench situated on the side of the street.

With the area being devoid of hostile bodies, another youth emerged from a nearby alleyway. He had black, curly hair that was a few inches long. He was about the same age as his acquaintance. Still sprawled out on the bench, the tired youth saw the other adolescent draw near. A look through the corner of the eye, a weak nod, breaths still coming fast. The curly-haired one circled around the occupied bench to stand beside his co-conspirator, who still tightly held the brown-skinned wallet.

"It better be worth it, Aram," said the young man to the one who came from the alleyway. He finally loosened his grip on the wallet to allow his friend to take hold of it. Aram dug through the folds and inserts of the stolen item like a raccoon going through a trash can.

"Well, Jo," began Aram, "I don't see a lot of plastic; but thankfully, he had a bunch of paper. We might get ten or twelve meals out of this one."

"Good," replied a still recuperating Joachim. Aram put the currency into his pocket and then tossed the wallet to the ground. He bent over Joachim and peered at him with amusement over his plight.

"Are you okay?"

"It's not the mileage; it's the speed," said Joachim, his breathing finally becoming normal.

"I can see that. But I mean, will you live?"

"Is that a serious question?" asked Joachim as he got to a sitting position on the bench.

"Do you really think I'm a serious person?"

"I guess you're right."

"It's been a long day."

"Funny, it went pretty fast for me," retorted an irritated Joachim, causing Aram to laugh while he sat down next to him on the bench.

"We need steady jobs," confessed Aram.

"Aram, do you really think we could find that?"

"Do you think that I think? It gives me headaches. Leave it to the people who can afford the medicine to think."

"I feel the same—just do and be merry," said Joachim. "That is how animals work, as I recall from my meager schooling."

"And I still remember the empty promises given that our lives would be so much better than before," recalled Aram.

"Maybe it's a case-by-case study."

"It's the soldiers, I tell you," said Aram in a conspiratorial tone. "If they weren't blockading most of the entrances to the proper territory, we would be able to get jobs in the city, live out here, and make the trek back-and-forth each day."

"Where did you get that idea?"

"I heard it on the radio. That Girgash man. He speaks the truth. If it wasn't for them, we could easily have good jobs."

"Instead, we steal from the rich."

"And give to the poor," said Aram, who got a perplexed look from Joachim. "That is, ourselves. We give to ourselves because we're poor."

"Yup."

"Well, since we have some money," began Aram, "how about we get some dinner for a change?"

"Sure. A big cheeseburger and fries sounds great right about now."

"Yeah."

Scene 6

The inn was a moderate structure with a moderate interior; neither elegant nor squalid. The lobby had some furniture gathered around two of its corners. Each set included two chairs, a couch, a small table, and an oriental rug. Lights were situated on the ceiling, providing sufficient sight for the space below. On the opposite end of the main entrance was the front desk, complete with a collection of door keys and mail slots. A single stairway led from that floor to the two floors above them.

Perziz Repha and David Shapsdale entered the sedate lobby. They bore their thick backpacks with weariness. Their appearance would have been more drastic were it not for the break in carrying the loads, courtesy Perziz's effort to scout out the inn before arriving. Mildly sweaty and unkempt, they walked toward the front desk unabated. They were the only souls within the lobby. There were no guests sitting at the furniture-laden corners nor visitors meandering about the floor. Not even the business section was occupied as the two journeymen approached the desk.

"Well, now I can see why you considered this a safe place," quipped David to Perziz, who granted him a wry smile. David then became professional. "What would you estimate as the probable population of this meager inhabitance?"

"I would venture to guess . . . around five thousand or so," responded Perziz, who was evidently looking up the stairway and balcony for any sign of life. There was no bell to alert the employees.

"So, if you consider the demographic required for fighting a war—the young adult male population—what number do you arrive to?"

"About six or seven hundred. Then again, they might be elsewhere about now. You know how many of these villages operate: full corroboration with the enemy of our people, and, in return, they get complete isolation from that foul pig-race."

"I see." David pondered. "Remind me why Moab wanted to establish a resistance stronghold here. I saw the exterior of Chaldea. In mere minutes, any besieging army could encircle and cut off water supplies. Then, they could easily storm the townhouses and destroy all resistance in an afternoon."

"Not if we can help it," countered Perziz.

"'Not if *I* can help it' might be the better term. That is why you gave me the gun out there, is it not? You wanted me to take that pistol from you; it was yours and Moab's will."

"Many would say it was God's will."

"I'll remember that tonight when I read, 'Thou shall not murder' in the Gideon."

"You miss the point, David," replied an annoyed Perziz.

"Not at all," David said in dramatic sarcasm, "for if I did, then how come vultures and serpents feast upon Girgash?"

And then, she entered from behind the desk. There was an office where she had previously been tending to some paperwork. She had brown hair tied together into a healthy, thick ponytail. There were some lighter streaks among the café hued mane; they looked either bleach blonde or maybe gray. Her face did not indicate an elderly age, though the lines around her eyes and neck showed one who had endured much. When she looked up to see the two men, her gaze was a mystical duo of sea green orbs. She faintly smiled before speaking, with David working to fix his hair and stature to make a positive impression.

"Hello, gentlemen," said the woman, her accent an exotic one. "How may I help you?"

"We have a reservation for a two-bedroom unit upstairs," replied Perziz. "You should find it under the name of Mohamed Said."

"Okay," she said, taking out a large book from under the front desk and opening it at the point where a red bookmark noted the latest entries.

"You are American, correct?" asked David.

"Born and raised," she said, emotionless.

"I have heard it's a fine country—full of cowboys and billionaires and quite possibly the most bizarre game of football I have ever seen."

She let out a quick laugh.

David was pleased that he could reach her spirits.

Getting to the correct page, she put on a pair of black-rimmed glasses to better examine the written text. After a few moments of searching, her index finger dragging down the page, she located the pseudonym. "Yes, there you are." She handed Perziz a pen and then turned the large book so that the text was right side-up for the two visitors. "If you could sign your name where it is printed, that would be much appreciated."

"Sure," obliged Perziz as he removed the cap from the pen and bent over to write down his faux signature.

"So, what brings you gentlemen to town?"

"Business," replied Perziz as he put the cap back onto the pen and placed it in the middle of the large, open book.

"Yes, a very noble business, in fact," added David.

"Really?"

"Why, yes."

"Our town could use some economic investment. What sort of business?"

"If my associate will permit, I shall explain."

"Not yet," stated Perziz.

"Then, so be it," said David, whose deliverance of the remark elicited a smile from the woman at the front desk.

"In due time, all will know," added Perziz.

"Okay, just curious," she said. "Anyhow, according to our records, you are prepaid for the next month. By then, if you're not out, you will be required to start paying."

"I'm certain our boss will make sure we stay longer."

"That's good. Anyway, laundry is on the basement level; television has basic cable; and you have one line for the internet and the phone."

"We shall be sure to choose wisely, then," said David, getting, to his delight, another smile from the woman.

"With all that said, I will now show you to your room. Please, follow me."

"A pleasure to do so."

Scene 7

Aram and Joachim entered their living space a few hours after David and Perziz entered the inn. Their place had its share of people lounging about. A few people were smoking cigarettes outside while a few more were smoking hookah inside. The two young men walked past their share of active and inactive people. Some played chess on cracked boards with damaged pieces; a couple of others were taking naps on worn couches. Still others were simply hanging around and engaging in idle chatter. It was not crowded, but it was populated. They walked to their apartment without interacting with the others. Up the stairs, up another flight, and then another.

Aram had the key and went ahead of Joachim, unlocking the door and walking in to let his friend catch it before it latched shut. Their abode was very much humble; it lacked a television or computer, central climate control, and much furniture. Only two simple cots for sleeping, two drawers for storing clothes, and a bathroom with a scattered array of basic toiletries. The corners had spiderwebs. Dirt and dust claimed spots all over the flooring. Unlike many evenings, they were going to bed with full stomachs thanks to the earlier thievery. They took turns getting ready for bed.

"I still say you should try being the runner for a change," shouted Joachim through the open bathroom door. He was just finishing up as Aram was laying down on his cot.

"I told you once; I tell you again. My lungs just don't like running."

"Oh, come on, it's been what? Two, three years since it happened?"

"Maybe three. Not sure," replied Aram. "But puking blood is not fun."

"There is that," conceded Joachim as he left the bathroom.

"Besides, another couple jobs like this one, and we might get enough money to live a little. Maybe move away to the city or something."

"We might not need to."

"What's that supposed to mean?" asked Aram, rising up from his cot.

"Well, I'm not sure."

"I'm like your brother; you have a problem telling me?"

"No," stated an annoyed Joachim. "Name one thing that I've ever held back from you."

"Very funny, like that would be possible."

"I'm not the kind of guy to deal in secrets; I was just gathering my thoughts, that's all," assured Joachim as he lay on his cot, his upper body shifted to look at his roommate.

"Yes, but still."

"Still, let's make this last conversation before bed worth anything, okay?" said Joachim, who then yawned.

"I didn't know any of our conversations had such value. Anyway, what is it that you were going to tell me that I kept claiming was a secret?"

"While running from the cops, this man helped me escape. He did so on the condition that I see him next morning."

"An employer?"

"Yeah, I think so."

"Did he look like a businessman?"

"Sort of. He seemed like he walked a long way, but he kept himself proper."

"Proper?"

"Yeah, proper," replied Joachim like he had figured something out. "I didn't catch his name, but he had a trusty look about him."

"Trusty look?"

"Yeah, you know, the caring, rich uncle look."

"I wouldn't know." Aram sighed. "My father was an only child."

"Still, I'm optimistic."

"I don't care what the experts say, that is the most dangerous job ever."

"What is?" asked Joachim, who figured out his own query. "Oh, you mean being optimistic."

"Yes, it's always dangerous, Jo. You ask for it when you think like that. Disappointment, thy name is optimist."

"Aram, my friend, I have had more disappointment as a pessimist than you could ever commit to admitting."

"Me, too."

"But now that I want to be an optimist, you tear me down."

"As a pessimist, I never get disappointed," said Aram, seemingly in prideful contentment.

"I can prove the opposite."

"Try me."

"Last winter regarding the heater."

"Hey, hey, I expected it to malfunction. My dismay came from it not working at all. This man, this mystery man . . . you think he will give me a job also?"

"Yeah, I think so."

"I doubt it," replied Aram as he leaned back into the cot and faced the ceiling with its myriad of cracks and dents.

"That's because you're a pessimist."

"No, that's because I'm a skeptic."

"Is that why you never go to that church to beg for alms?"

"No, that is because on some days I never want to wake up, and those days are many."

"I'll remember that."

"No, you won't," said Aram through a yawn. "You never remember such things. Your pea-brain is as small as mine. Must be malnutrition."

Joachim yawned again. "Or lack of sleep."

"Good night, then," said Aram, who closed his eyes and turned away from his friend. Joachim shifted his upper body to face the cracked ceiling.

"Good night, yesterday," he declared to himself in a voice not loud enough to wake his roommate. "And a welcome to marvelous, glowing amber day, still preparing in the swamp, black night."

SCENE 8

Rest was brief for David Shapsdale and Perziz Repha. The room for the temporary respite was a respectable one. Clean and furnished, it was pristine for want of guests. It had two full-sized beds and an artificial climate control system. There was also a full bathroom and a kitchen space that included a refrigerator and freezer. For David, it was the largest unit he had ever lived in as an adult. Rather than revel in such a triumph, he and his traveling companion set about their work of making Chaldea a bastion of resistance.

As the sun was setting, a local business sold the duo a computer, scanner, and printer while another merchant sold them some office furniture. The woman at the front desk looked on with amazement and brimming curiosity as the various things were sent up the stairs and toward the recently occupied guest room. As David organized the furniture, Perziz put together the technological devices; he had a greater literacy with such mechanical items, screwing in cables, connecting lines, powering up the machine, creating screennames and passwords, and a host of other matters.

"You young people and your technology," joked David to Perziz while the latter was working on the monitor. Perziz briefly smiled, evidently aware of the fact that Shapsdale was only two years older than himself. They were in the living room of the unit. It was biggest room of the three and included the kitchen space. David was leaning against the back of the couch, which was facing the cube-shaped television.

"It's not the best connection to the internet, but it will do," explained Perziz as he continued to stare at the bright screen of the beige box monitor. "This will help us grow our online presence."

"My apologies for being made just a little lower than the angels"—David approached a seated Perziz still focusing on the screen—"but what good does that do us?"

"You are not familiar with the concept of social media? Message boards? Email chains? Blogs and bloggers?"

"No, no, maybe, not really, and no," replied David.

"This, David, is going to help us spread the word. It is the greatest means of advancing ideas since the printing press."

"Okay," said David with an open mind. "So, if you have this better printing press, why do you need me, and why are we here?"

"Recruitment, of course," responded Perziz. "We cannot win this war only in the cyber-world. We must win it in the real world."

"I see."

"So, starting tomorrow, we will need to start getting young men to join our ranks. From there, I will oversee their basic training; and then we will loose them upon the military."

"Then, you should be happy to know that I have found a fellow who might be able to help," said David, finally prompting Perziz to turn away from the screen.

"Who would that be?"

"Some young thief. We discoursed a little while you were verifying the security of this place. We will meet him tomorrow morning.

Hopefully, he shall be a conduit to get other young men into our little parade of effort."

"Sounds promising," said Perziz. He exited out of the web page and then got up to exit the living room. "Now, if you will excuse me, I must make a call."

"Just as well," noted David. "I just realized the hour is getting late, and I need to do a couple of things myself." Both men went to the bedroom where the unit's only landline phone was located. David went to the bathroom, which was connected to the bedroom, carrying a small bag of toiletries while Perziz picked up the receiver and dialed a number.

"Hello, switchboard?" inquired Perziz. "Yes, I want to make a long-distance call . . . The villa of Moab. I believe the address is . . . Oh, okay, you know him as well . . . Who will be paying?" Perziz thought a while and smiled. "He will, of course."

As Perziz waited for the call to go through, David removed his shirt. He washed his upper body and then proceeded to shave with a two-bladed razor. He also added deodorant and flossed his teeth. Returning to the bedroom, he opened his backpack to find a new T-shirt and a button-up outer shirt to wear for the evening.

"Hello?" inquired Perziz on the phone after he heard noise on the other end of the line. "Yes, I hear you, um, Vesuvius . . . Yes, the crucifixion went as planned . . . One thief did not make it. Which one survived? Why"—Perziz looked at David, who had put on the T-shirt and was taking hold of the outer shirt with both hands—"why, the one on the right side made it, for he was on the right hand of God . . . True, Vesuvius, very true . . . When can I expect an eruption?" Perziz seemed confused by David putting on the formal shirt and then taking a tie from his things. The dialogue continued.

"Your predictions state no time in the future. Well, that is very good news . . . Yes, Vesuvius, the village is growing . . . By next week, expect Pompeii to be in position. Yes, no one wants an eruption either. Goodbye!" Perziz hung up the phone and immediately turned to David. "Where are you going?"

"To further investigate a matter," commented David as he lifted up his collar and looped the tie over his neck, already in a Windsor knot.

"What matter would that happen to be?"

"Esther."

"Who?"

"The woman who oversees the affairs of the inn," replied David as he took a dark blue dinner jacket from the backpack.

"I did not know she even gave her name. I must not have been paying attention," confessed Perziz.

"That is the difference between myself and you and Moab. You two look upon those beneath you with contempt and insignificance, I do not."

"That is a matter of opinion. Not every man who is well off that forgets a name does so out of classist enmity."

"Let me ask you something. What is that whole 'eruption' and 'Vesuvius' stuff you were going on about? I know you were calling Moab about something."

"For now, I can say that it is nothing that concerns you. Your occupation shall be to rally those many potential soldiers; and I, in turn, give them weapons."

"Who trains them?"

"I already told you, I will."

"You said basic training. Our enemies have more than that."

"You overestimate their abilities, David," said Perziz, brushing off his comment. "In this land, everyone knows how to use a weapon. So, it won't take much to mount resistance."

"Then, we will lose."

"Defeatist attitudes are an especial pet peeve for me, David Shapsdale. Is our benevolence so invisible to you that you do not see the sheer improbability of failure?"

"There is no way that we can match them gun for gun, much less training for training with *your* attitude," countered David.

"Maybe you are correct. Conventional war would doom us unless there could be proper training for a modern conflict. I will see to that."

"Don't you mean 'Vesuvius' will see to that?"

"Nevertheless, David, there is still the issue of further recruitment."

"That issue I will talk with you about when I return from my outing with Esther," said David as he reentered the bathroom to look at himself in the mirror.

"Are you that determined?" asked an amused Perziz.

"Are you married?" asked David through the open bathroom door.

"Yes, I am," replied Perziz as David returned to the bedroom.

"Then you have no idea what it's like to be my age and still be single."

"David, you are not even in your fortieth winter!"

"Truly, but that cold day comes closer and closer every minute," stated David as he exited the bedroom, turning his back on a visibly amused Perziz.

Scene 9

David walked down the stairs of the hotel, encountering none of the other guests. He reached the foyer without problem. The room was quiet, but not vacant. There were two young men, both with dark hair and mustaches, who were sitting in two chairs in the far corner of the chamber. They took a passing look at David, then kept looking at the front desk. David turned his attention there as well; and a few moments later, Esther appeared, her hair fashioned into a ponytail. She adjusted her glasses to look down at some written records, seeming to verify a few things. Without speaking, David drew near and, resting his left arm on the counter, got her attention.

"Good evening," she said to him.

"Good evening," he replied, sounding bashful. "Are you ready?"

"Just about," she said, closing a book and putting it under the desktop. "Give me a few more moments."

"By all means."

Esther went back into the small office adjoining the reception area, likely to finish with a few other things. David waited, casually looking about the waiting room while doing so. He noticed that the two men were staring at him. No sign of malice, but no sign of joy, either. David kept turning his head, pretending to not notice that they kept looking at him. He was feeling a bit awkward, but the two men did nothing more than look. Whatever anxiety they gave him evaporated when Esther returned, her glasses put away so that he could perfectly view her sea green eyes.

"Now, I'm ready," she said. She looked at the two men in the corner, then back to David. "You should leave first. I will be there shortly."

"Okay," said David, who obeyed despite his confusion.

Chaldea was quieter in the evening. Many of the folks who were there during the day resided in smaller villages and communities scattered around the desert region. It was a place of work—especially the vineyards, which produced the wine that helped keep the community economically viable. As David paced about the outside of the hotel, the most prominent noise emanated from the minarets as the calls to prayer were hollered in euphony.

After about a minute, Esther left the hotel. She was modestly dressed, with a simple gown that covered her arms and legs but was not constraining.

"I am not taking you away from prayers, am I?"

"Nope," said David.

"Before we go anywhere," she said with great seriousness, "you should know I'm a widow. That is why those men were staring at us. They are my late husband's cousins."

"I see."

"If that's not okay with you—"

"No, no, I am okay," said David, who smiled. "I guess the Western side of my heritage really shines on this part."

She smiled.

"So, um, where to?"

"The outskirts," Esther replied. "I love to be there. It is so peaceful."

"Lead the way," David said.

It did not take them long to go beyond the buildings of that humble town, the wailing from the minarets still in their ears. They even saw the occasional person along the road on a carpet and bowing toward Mecca. The evening was serene, with no clouds and a nice mild breeze. Esther looked at the stars. They were easy to chart in the absence of urban interference. As they got passed the last of the structures, Esther seemed quite distracted by the constellations above the two. David was amused.

"Do you look to the stars for justification?"

"I need no justification from bodies that can never give it," she replied.

"How do you know that?"

"Stars are just balls of gas, hydrogen, and helium. They vary in size, but even the smallest could swallow this planet whole," said Esther in a matter-of-fact tone. "They are so little from here, like the lighthouses' warnings from the ocean's breast."

"So the stars can provide warning," David commented.

"Are you a philosopher?"

"When it calls for it."

"I could never stand philosophy; I always got poor grades in it back at school."

"How come?"

"Because, David," said Esther, "philosophy is the territory men flee to once they have lost the battles for history, logic, mathematics, and science."

"Ouch," commented an amused David.

"That would be the pain of history, logic, mathematics, and science bearing down on that last bulwark of yours, David. What is your last name?"

"Shapsdale. You can still call me David."

"I prefer David," agreed Esther. "There is a certain appropriate ring to it, given the history of this land."

"This was a good grade for you in school, I assume."

"Everything but philosophy," she noted.

"Well, I am always willing to help with that," David said. "After all, 'the life which is unexamined is not worth living.'"

"That sounds familiar," she said, looking at David. "I know I have heard that before."

"Socrates," David informed her. "He had his moments, you must admit."

"I guess he did," she remarked. "So you were educated in the West?"

"Yes. My beloved father made sure of it. He wanted me to be a good Englishman."

"How well did it take?"

David laughed. "Well, at the least, I liked all the books I got to read. They were my favorite part of my occidental education."

"Have you ever been to the United States?"

"No," began David, who then gave a smile that appeared conniving. "However, I have read your literature. Your Irving is an amusing fellow, and your Twain and Steinbeck portray life better than any history textbook. And Faulkner's plots were jigsaws."

"They were," Esther said, laughing. "It took me a few reads to understand *Light in August*. And I gave up on *The Sound and the Fury* halfway through."

"I preferred *Absalom, Absalom,* myself."

"To be honest, though, I always preferred the older English works, those written long, long ago, before there was an American Republic."

"Chaucer?"

"He was okay," she said.

"The Venerable Bede?"

"I thought he was decent. A good historian overall," replied Esther. She seemed to be testing the depth of his knowledge when she asked, "What did you think of Eric Arthur Blair?"

"Of the many British authors, I rarely read Orwell."

"How about the Bard?"

"Yes, he was my favorite."

"How come?"

"He was able to mix poetry and realism all in one dosage of writing."

"Good point. I also liked Shakespeare. Except, I must confess, that he had my approval for different reasons," Esther said.

"Really? What made you approve of him?"

"I always liked his fools and clowns."

"An interesting choice. How come?"

"They always said the smartest things. The main characters were always stuck in a fantasy world, with monologues about obscure references to every other extinct pagan deity. But the fools and the clowns, they were realists. They were actually smarter than the people who were over them. Let's say, I sympathize."

"My condolences, then," said David. "Do you live in a Shakespearian tragedy?"

Esther looked deeply into his eyes. "I was until tonight."

David reciprocated the intimate stare, the peaceful examination of the sea green circles before him. "Did little, old me with my minor words of arrogant banter play a great role in making that possible?"

"No one talks to me around here, David, no one. I am a stranger, a widow, and in my thirties. I only ever get business exchanges. Little else."

"A slim number of friends."

"Strangers are frowned upon here."

"That happens often."

"Where does all the hate come from?"

"Is it not obvious?" David questioned, glancing at her.

"The soldiers, I assume."

"Yes, them."

"Them?" asked a concerned, yet still intimate, Esther. "You use exclusionary words. Surely, they have not treated your people any worse than the last country to rule over your land with an iron fist."

"That doesn't make the oppression any less iron in density," grumbled David. "Their very presence here in my country is damaging. I and my friends, my countrymen . . . we're going to kick them out. By whatever means is proper and necessary."

"All because their military uses this region as a buffer for confirmed enemies?" asked Esther. She bit her lower lip while David kept his temper, for he realized that she did not mean to offend.

"You got your answer about where the hate comes from. A pity it had to extend to you. Let me apologize on behalf of my race for any who may have hated you because of them."

"I accept your apology," she said, lightly. "You must be the first person I've talked to for this long about something other than business in months."

"Happy to do the task," said David with renewed joy. "The pleasure was mine also, of course."

Esther smiled at the comment and then yawned. "Sorry, sorry, it's not you." She laughed, evidently embarrassed.

"Understood, understood," said David, who smiled with both hands raised as though to calm a situation.

"It was a long day, a long week, and it's already late," she said with another quick laugh. "I guess I have been staring at the stars for too long."

"Evenings I've wasted many times without sleep, my dear," said David. "This evening, I could care less about resting my eyes."

She smiled at him.

"Maybe more light will come to the future in your skies, stargazer."

"It's called the dawn, my David," said Esther as the two drew closer.

Their intimacy was disrupted by musical noises from within Chaldea. Instruments played festive beats, voices eventually adding poetic sentences to the melodies. Esther and David awkwardly smiled at each other over the interruption.

"That usually happens this time of week," Esther explained. "After the prayers are over, everyone gets to partying."

David got to a proper posture and then took the hand of his female company. "Good lady, may I on this most pleasant evening have the pleasure of a dance?"

"David"—she laughed, initially nodding her head in the negative—"I don't know how to dance. I am a wallflower, through and through."

"And I am only good at slow dances, so we will do what we can," insisted David.

Esther changed her nod to an affirmative and got up, still holding his left hand.

"Fine, kind sir. Your request is granted," she said, smiling while clearly suppressing laughter. "So, now what do we do?"

"I know the beat is quick, but how about we go the usual slow route?"

"Sounds good," replied Esther, as the two moved closer together.

David put his right hand on her lower back while she took hold of his upper back. The two began to sway in the desert clearing, both fighting off laughter at their efforts at civilization.

"You know; you are not half bad."

"I will take whatever compliment I can," she said. A moment of seriousness entered her. "What if the village folk see us doing this? They do not care much for an unrelated man and woman touching each other."

"Let them talk," insisted David. "And we strangers will dance in the darkness."

SCENE 10

"I am thankful to whatever Master of the universe exists that our landlord's daughter makes breakfast for us," stated Aram as he and Joachim were walking to the previously agreed upon meeting place.

"She seems to exclude everyone else, if you've noticed," noted Joachim. The two were side by side, walking along a sparsely populated sidewalk. At that hour, most everyone was at work or still at home. Markets and open-air shops were on other streets.

"Maybe she has taken a liking to us, Jo," agreed Aram.

"Decent, Christian woman of high moral fiber falls for the lowly, thieving tramp. Sounds like a clichéd love story."

"It's a reasoning."

"It's a flawed reasoning."

"You do not reason as I reason."

"You admit often to not using your mind to think," said Joachim as they got within sight of the hookah bar.

"True," conceded Aram. "Thinking gives me pain, but I sometimes indulge."

"I can imagine. Is your pea-brain working now?"

"Yes, it is." Aram nodded. "And it is telling me that this is a bad idea."

"The meeting?"

"Yes, the meeting," said Aram as he stopped within a few feet of the bar's entrance, prompting Joachim to do likewise. "This stranger you talk so highly about."

"The trusty one?"

"Yes, the trusty one."

"He's like a rich uncle, I can tell already."

"Why did you have to bring me along?"

"You keep asking that question. You're only going to get the same answer."

"Tell me again. For my pea-brain."

"He's a businessman, and he wants as much help as possible."

"But you don't even know what he wants!" declared an exasperated Aram.

"Manpower. That is what he wants."

"You sure?"

"Any proof to the contrary?"

"No, but still—"

"Come on," urged Joachim, taking Aram by the arm.

While his friend was still nervous, he nonetheless allowed Joachim to drag him into the hookah bar. As with the street, there was little activity within the darker space. The interior featured a paneled dance floor at the center with eight booths along the walls. Each booth had leather seats and a prominently placed hookah stand. Two of the booths had a few people in them, putting the tip of the hose into their mouths, inhaling, and then blowing forth smoke.

Despite the dim lighting, Joachim quickly spotted the businessman and another gentleman. When the former looked at in their general direction and saw them, he smiled and waved.

"No turning back," confidently stated Joachim to Aram, finally letting go of his arm.

"I hate you, Jo."

"Hatred is for the weak-minded."

"What do you think I am?" Aram rhetorically inquired as the two walked toward the corner booth where the two strangers were seated. Aram noticed that the hookah station was removed from the table. Instead, there was an opened bottle of Chaldean red wine, a carafe of water, two filled wine glasses, and two empty cylindrical water glasses.

"Greetings again, Joachim," said the businessman, smiling. "I am David Shapsdale. You are both free to call me David. In fact, I prefer it." Aram and Joachim took turns shaking hands with David, with Aram introducing himself.

"And this is my associate, Mr. Perziz Repha. Honestly, I am not sure what he wants to be called."

"Nothing savage, of course," said Perziz as he stood and shook hands with the two youths. He sat back down on the far right of the booth, with David on his left.

"Go ahead and sit down; I think we are all friends now," said David, with Joachim sitting to his left and Aram ending on the far left of the booth. "Care for some water? I am assuming you are both too new an age for an adult beverage."

"You're right about that," said Joachim as he was about to go for the carafe. David beat him to it and poured the drinks.

"Now, now, allow me," insisted David. "He who wants to lead must be willing to serve."

"Sounds biblical."

"Pretty sure it is," said David as he put the carafe back at the center table. "And if it is not, then it should be." The comment made all at the table either smile or laugh. "Now to business. My associate Perziz and I would like to employ the two of you. We are trying to build something important in Chaldea. Something we expect will spread throughout the entire occupied land."

"If you want to open a vineyard, you're going to get a lot of competition," said Aram.

"I do not want to open a vineyard, Aram; I have another plan."

"What do you mean?"

"I feel like I can trust both of you. Indeed, I feel like I can trust everyone in this village with what I must tell you."

"Okay," Aram nervously stated.

"Our business is that of liberation—liberation for Chaldea, for this occupied region, maybe even for all people. After all, an injustice somewhere is an injustice everywhere."

"That's not biblical, is it?"

"Regardless," interjected Perziz, his voice becoming softer as he continued speaking, "what Mr. Shapsdale is trying to say is that we are part of the resistance movement. We want to kick the military out, and you can help us."

"How?" asked a surprised Joachim.

"Perziz will train you in the art of guerilla warfare. You will be armed; and when possible, you will attack soldiers."

"Wait a minute, wait a minute," said Aram, lowering his voice and waving a hand around. "You want us to kill people? Like, people— *human beings* people?"

"That is what resistance movements do, last I checked," said David.

"I don't know about that."

"Remember who you are dealing with, Aram and Joachim. These are the people who are depriving you of your right to self-determination."

"Self-determin—what?"

"Self-determination, Joachim. The ability to determine your future without anyone stopping you from doing so," explained David. "You don't want to spend your whole life running from the police, do you?"

"No, I guess not."

"You want to be part of something bigger, yes?"

"Yes."

"Then what is the problem?"

"Killing people," insisted Joachim, who was looking down at his glass of water. "I mean, I don't like them, either. But still. Still. They have families."

"Rodents have families," David sternly stated.

"True," replied Joachim.

"There is that," agreed Aram.

"If it makes you feel better," began David, "you will only be killing soldiers. Men in uniform. People who chose to oppress us."

"That is true," said Joachim.

"Reminds me of the stuff that Girgash used to say on the radio," said Aram, who was almost convinced. "My buddies and I—we used to always listen to him. He was an inspiration."

"Then it will break your heart to know that the military just killed him," said David, getting a look of shock from all three of the men seated with him.

"What? I thought they just ended his radio program," said a wide-eyed Aram.

"Oh no, that was not enough for them," continued David, with Perziz biting his lip. "They shot him dead in the desert—execution style, right in the chest."

"Wait a minute, wait a minute," began Joachim. "Why haven't we heard anything from the news about this?"

"Because it happened only yesterday. I know about it because Perziz and I were on our way here and we saw it. Quite terrifying, really. I assure you, someone will find his body; and the truth will be revealed soon. But you heard it here first."

David watched his companions carefully, as Perziz's face betrayed that he was both impressed and unnerved by David's willingness to fabricate details. Fortunately, David saw that Aram and Joachim were too distracted by his claim to notice.

"Wow, unbelievable," said an astonished Aram.

David watched as their astonishment converted to anger, and from anger came resolve.

"Sign me up. I want to fight them."

"The same with me. I'll sign up."

"Good, good," said David, patting Joachim on the shoulder. "You two have the honor of being our first recruits."

"But you cannot be the only ones," added Perziz. "We need to have as many young men as we can to fight the occupation."

"That won't be hard," said Aram. "Jo and I know a bunch of kids from the mosques. They don't like the military either, and they aren't employed."

"And they used to listen to Girgash all the time," Joachim added.

"That sounds very promising," said Perziz.

"I think we can drink to this glorious future," said David.

The other three obliged, lifting their drinks.

David gave a conniving grin at the prospects of that meeting and what came of it. His elevated glass gently tapped the sides of the other three glasses, and all four drank either water or wine that morning in celebration of a promising start.

Scene 11

Corporal Ruth Greenberg and Private Shiri Dahan were coming from another false alarm. Earlier that day, Greenberg had received a phone call from a checkpoint: a traveler whose behavior was labeled suspicious. Like a fire department getting an emergency alert, Greenberg and Dahan quickly gathered their things and rushed to the facility connected to the checkpoint. The person of interest was detained. However, after an hour-long interrogation, Greenberg found little amiss about the detained individual. With some apologies granted, the sojourner was allowed to enter the country.

On the way back to the office, Greenberg took a call on her cellular phone. Greenberg rarely used the device, and few people had her number. Shiri did not even own a mobile device, instead having a pager to keep track of messages. Just as the uppermost floors of the facility were visible, Greenberg had the jeep turn to go to a different destination. Several minutes later, the two military personnel were at a city morgue. Without explaining the details of the phone call, Greenberg stopped the jeep and got out. Shiri followed suit, having to rush at first to keep up with her superior.

"Corporal Greenberg, why are we at a civilian morgue?" asked Shiri as the two neared the glass doors.

"A friend of mine works here as a coroner," Greenberg replied stoically as she and Shiri each pushed open a door to enter the facility. "He told me he found something that I might find interesting."

"Okay, what is it?"

"Something that could not be explained over the phone," said Greenberg, getting a nod of acceptance from Shiri.

The two approached the front desk and signed into the guest list. There was brief conversation between Shiri's superior officer and the receptionist. Both being in uniform and Greenberg being familiar to the staff helped expedite their trip to the interior. From there, the two went down a short hall and then down two flights of stairs. They then entered a large, cooled room where the dead were preserved. The walls contained the reflective silver drawers that had slabs bearing bodies of various people. Inhabitants of the room were largely elderly, and their fates came through natural causes. The living person in the room was a middle-aged man with tan skin, dark hair, glasses, and a thick beard.

"Salaam, Ahmed," said Greenberg, giving a big smile at the sight of the coroner. This was the first time Shiri had seen her superior act in such a sociable manner.

"As-Salaam-Alaikum." The coroner smiled. "How are you doing, Ruth?"

"Fine. Busy, but all right."

"That is good," said Ahmed. "And your father?"

"The usual."

"Of course," said Ahmed, briefly laughing.

"And this is my new subordinate, Private Shiri Dahan."

"A pleasure," said Ahmed.

Shiri smiled and nodded, aware as her superior was about the customary interactive rules between the sexes.

"You said you had something interesting for me—something that might be too sensitive to talk over the phone about."

"Yes, I do," said Ahmed as he beckoned the two soldiers over to one of the closed compartments on the wall. "A few Arab boys were skipping class today. While venturing around the dunes, they stumbled upon a corpse."

"That will teach them to play hooky," commented Greenberg. "So why did you think this one might be of interest to me?"

"Well, my grandfather used to always say that 'showing is better than telling.'"

Ahmed pulled back the drawer, revealing a body covered in a white sheet that lay on the slab.

While Greenberg remained firm, Shiri was a little uncomfortable. Aside from a few family funerals in her youth, she had never found herself so close to a deceased figure.

Greenberg and Dahan took a couple of steps backward while Ahmed walked around to the edge of the sheet and dragged it off the face. There was some mutilation, some of the flesh having been consumed by animals. However, the countenance remained unmistakable.

"Look familiar?" he asked.

"Girgash Keniz," replied Greenberg.

"Correct. I did some DNA analysis to double-check; but yes; it's him."

"Who is he?" Shiri sincerely asked.

"She's new," explained Greenberg to Ahmed.

"That's understandable. If you don't follow politics, especially crazy dissidents like Keniz, you would be ignorant about him. Truth be told, we'd probably all be a little better off if everyone was ignorant of him."

"He was a firebrand, constantly attacking the merits of the occupation," added Greenberg to Shiri. She then returned her attention to Ahmed. "How did he die?"

"A bullet to the heart. I removed the slug. The caliber looks to be fairly small, just large enough to kill someone at close range."

"I see," said Greenberg as she looked over the corpse. "Thanks for letting me know about this, Ahmed."

"My pleasure."

"I am going to make a call to headquarters, and they will pick up the body. They will need all the paperwork from your autopsy."

"Of course," replied Ahmed. "I've been through this cycle before."

Greenberg looked at her phone. "I'm not getting a signal down here, so until next time."

"My family is having a neighborhood outing," said Ahmed, changing the subject with a smile. "You and your father should come. We'll be serving kosher, so everyone should be safe."

"I will let him know," Greenberg said as she began to exit. "Salaam."

"Salaam," replied Ahmed as the two soldiers departed.

"So, this is a big deal?" asked Shiri as the two exited the morbid chamber.

"Very. Especially since Keniz was one of the few occupation critics who had broad support among both Christians and Muslims."

"Permission to speak freely, Corporal?"

"What did I tell you before?" inquired a clearly annoyed Greenberg.

"Well, this query is a little iffy. I mean, not to be troubling, but are we sure that we—you know, our side—didn't kill him? With him silent, that is one less troublemaker."

"Private Dahan"—Greenberg abruptly stopped between the two flights of stairs—"I can assure you that we did not. Do you, a recent graduate of the academy, know why?"

"Why?" asked Shiri.

"Because there are two ways in which we engage in anti-personnel attacks. One is to launch an airstrike, and the other is to have a sniper pick them off. It obviously was not the former. As for the latter, snipers aim for the head—and at a distance."

"Good point," agreed Shiri.

"When the news gets out, there will be those who will claim we did it. I am just thankful that these rumors will be regionally restricted."

"Yes, Corporal," said Shiri, again playing catchup as Greenberg ascended the staircase. As they exited the building, Shiri had a thought. "I have to wonder, though, Corporal. Maybe this is a non-political act. Maybe someone just wanted to kill Keniz for no reason other than a thrill or a bad robbery."

Greenberg looked at her subordinate coldly. "Need I remind you, Private Dahan, that just because there's a God in Heaven doesn't mean there isn't a devil in Hell?"

"Understood, Corporal," responded Shiri as they opened the doors to the jeep.

"Good."

Scene 12

"'Philosophy is the territory that men flee to when they have lost the battles for history, logic, mathematics, and science,'" quoted David as he sat down opposite Joachim in the study room of his penthouse apartment. He took a swig from his wine glass, gently tipping the stem to let the crimson contents enter his mouth. The taste and the smell of the wine returned him back to the old country. The words returned him to her. First came the happiness of the memories, then the pain, and then he came back to that late hour.

"Was that Yeats, King, or Wiesel?" asked Joachim.

Minutes earlier, Joachim had decided to leave his seat and walk around the study. He took some seconds to investigate the various authors and titles on the shelves placed throughout the chamber. David noticed that, for a fleeting moment, his visitor's eye had been off the firearm. However, before he could act, Joachim turned back to look at David and the small table, where the weapon was resting.

"None of those brilliant minds devised such a quote. Rather, they were the words of a good friend," responded David.

"Esther?"

David looked up at the standing Joachim. He was on the other side of the small table, over him with a proper posture. Only his neck was bent so that his eyes could better see the man who had hosted the party. "Yes, her. You met her, the American innkeeper."

"You must have annoyed every nationalist by your friendship with her."

"Hardly," said David. "Moab had cousins living in the United States. Perziz was moving to that very country the last I heard." David looked down at the glass and caressed the bulb of the glass before looking back at his company. "To speak no untruth, Joachim, the only race we—and that includes you, by the way—ever hated were those vermin. You do remember hating them also, correct?"

"Yes, I remember the dogmas you implanted in my mind," recounted Joachim. "So no one cared, not even Moab?"

"Esther was practically one of us; she really was," began David, a little weaker in controlling his emotion than before. "She knew the culture, the language. She was a survivor, like me. However, she was better at it than me, since at least my hostile dwellings had the same tongue and foundation. Not her—she had to endure and prevail over so much. I hated what happened to her."

"And what did happen to her?" asked Joachim, yet David suspected that he already knew the answer.

"Do you remember when I first introduced her to the others?" asked David with a sudden sound of gaiety, causing Joachim to give a wry smile and direct his eyes downward. "To you and even some of the other guerillas in our cause?" David laughed while Joachim remained proper in temperament and posture. "Some of you claimed that we acted enough alike that we had to be family."

"Yes, I remember," Joachim humored. "I urged you on more than one occasion to get a blood test and some papers on lineage. For all we knew, you were distant cousins."

"I think everyone knew that our homologies were merely an extension of proof that we were meant to be together. Perziz agreed with the idea. I liked Perziz—eventually, anyway. He was an acquired taste, but I liked him."

"I already ran into him . . . he will deceive no longer," Joachim flatly stated.

David took another drink from his glass. "Tragic."

"Necessary," countered Joachim, his voice becoming more passionate as he continued speaking. "I know you think I am still the feeble-minded creature you first encountered in Chaldea, but you will suppress the thought. Turn the tongue and change the subjects, over and over, trying to recollect when and where, anything to set forth some distraction. No one will let you prevail this time, David. No one is going to come to your aid; soon enough, you will be carried cold out of this room."

"The greatest inevitability," commented David, moving his glass in a small circular motion.

"It is not, by the way."

"You know, Joachim," began David, ignoring the bizarre remark that his company made that echoed his earlier comments. "I must confess that your grip on the gun is loose. Right now, in fact, you have already stopped looking at it as I talk to you."

Joachim quickly turned his gaze to the small table and found the weapon right where he had put it earlier.

"In time, I can easily distract you well enough to launch myself toward that gun and then take it as my own."

Joachim gave a hapless smirk in response.

"You shall not be able to murder me before I get that gun safely into my hands."

"That is my intention," immediately replied Joachim.

David was fully perplexed. "Excuse me?"

"I am consistent in my words, David," explained Joachim. "You see, when I told you of the others and how none of them are alive, I told no lie. They are dead, but I did not kill them."

"Even my intellect fails to understand," said David, placing his glass onto the small table, mere inches from the firearm.

"I will tell you of your evils, deceiver, and you will realize what you have done," declared Joachim.

David interrupted. "I could easily make a valiant struggle, even with cannon to the left, right, and center of me, going into the valley of thunder."

"However, your mental strength will not last so long. Alas, you miss the point," said Joachim, whose next sentence stunned David to silence. "I have no intention of killing you. By the end of this conversation, you will take the gun into your hands . . . and kill yourself."

INTERMISSION

ACT III

SCENE 1

Aram and Joachim waited inside a building across from the restaurant. They were not in Chaldea but another, smaller village located closer to the border. It was a stricter society, where all the women wore hijabs and all businesses closed for prayers. With the exception of the restaurant that the two young men were scouting, no facility was allowed to serve or possess alcohol. The natives looked upon Aram and Joachim with inherent suspicion, most likely because neither was particularly religious. Many helping the two youths saw little wrong with executing people for apostasy. Violence between them would likely ensue, were it not for the immediate presence of a mutual enemy.

It was an apartment complex. The trappings were similar to where Aram and Joachim lived, with basic heating and air conditioning, squalid quarters, and little more than cots within each unit. They were in the lobby, which was a drab light brown akin to the dunes surrounding the village. Three framed calligraphic art pieces were hung on the walls. In one corner, there was a collection of prayer rugs, as well as two shelves where the devout were expected to place their shoes when praying. The complex had three public bathrooms, each of which had shower areas for wudu. As with the average Western hotel room having a Gideon, each bedroom had a copy of the Qur'an.

Bland curtains covered the two windows placed between the main entrance. Aram and Joachim were seated by the window to the left of the door. They took turns watching the restaurant. While it was the dinner hour, it was clear that neither youth was hungry. The nerves bound within each was sufficient to deter the innate urge for food. They sat at two chairs without cushions at a small round table. Their weapons, loaded and ready, lay upon the table's wooden surface. There were three guns altogether; two pistols and one assault rifle. The former were single-action 9 mm calibers that each had a three-dot sight. The black-colored weapons were commonly used by local law enforcement. In fact, those two were given to them by local police. In case it was necessary, the two had a Kalashnikov as well. Like the pistols, the Kalashnikov was given to them by the villagers, specifically a gentleman who had fought against the occupiers a generation ago as part of a Jihadist militia.

"Any sign of them?" Aram asked Joachim. Evidently, the curly-haired youth had developed a way to somehow be bored and nervous simultaneously.

Joachim was looking outside the window, his hand holding back one of the curtains.

"Nope."

"They're coming, right?"

"That's what we were told."

"Then, where are they?" asked a frustrated Aram.

"Well, I can tell you where they aren't."

Aram sighed. "Did I mention how uncomfortable these chairs are?"

"Several times."

"Oh, okay. Well, these chairs are very uncomfortable. They're like—"

"Sleeping on a rock," completed Joachim, conveying a degree of annoyance equal to his peer. "I know. You don't need to repeat it."

"What else can I do?"

"Get up and walk around," replied Joachim, still eyeing the front of the restaurant.

"Fine, then." Aram rose from his chair and paced a few steps. "When do we call it a night and go back?"

"Are you nervous?"

"Why do you ask that?"

"Because you sound like you want them to not show up."

"Well," began Aram, shifting awkwardly. "Not to sound uncommitted or nothing, but you know, this is kind of new to me."

"You mean, killing people?"

"Yeah."

"I understand. I've never killed a person before."

"Then, you'd be happy if they didn't show either, right?" asked Aram.

"Between you and me . . . yes. Yes, I would. I'd like it if they didn't show. I'd like it if they all went home. Then we can go home. Everyone can go home."

"But our home stinks."

"I know that, Aram," replied Joachim. "But it's better than being away."

"Maybe."

Joachim jumped in his seat. "Here they come," he whispered.

Aram rushed to the window and looked through the small opening between the curtains.

The lights around the restaurant showed the three figures. Each wore an olive green uniform, black boots, and black berets. They lacked any chevrons, implying a lack of ranked importance. They engaged in lighthearted banter, oblivious to the eyes leering at them from across the street.

"Okay, it's happening," said Aram as he and Joachim gathered their weapons and themselves. "This is actually happening."

"Remember, we have to wait a few minutes before going in," cautioned Joachim. "The owner said he'd send someone out for us."

"Okay, okay," said Aram as he breathed nervously. "I am ready."

"Let's get into place," said Joachim.

The two armed youths exited the apartment complex.

A few people saw them going across the street. However, there was no fear; everyone in that small community knew what Aram and Joachim were about to do. One of the locals passing by the duo even gave them a smile of appreciation.

After getting across the street, the two huddled along the side of the restaurant. The windows had colored stained glass, making it hard for patrons to get a good look of the outside. They were there for what felt like hours—yet was only five minutes.

A male patron exited the restaurant. He had a thick beard and wore a taqiyah skullcap. Upon looking at the two armed young men, he showed no trepidation but rather nodded.

"You know what to do," he said, then casually walked away.

Without further delay, Aram and Joachim entered the restaurant. Both youths had their pistols drawn; and Aram had the assault rifle slung on his back, just in case. Entering the interior, they found few people around other than the three soldiers. They were still in a pleasant mood, each with a glass of water. They had ordered their main course. Unbeknownst to the soldiers, the kitchen staff made no effort to cook their meals.

Just as one of them was starting to look in the direction of the duo, the youths raised their pistols and opened fire. The shots were wild, hitting the bodies of the trio, the chairs, and the nearby wall. Blood tarnished the three olive green uniforms, with two of the three being dead within moments of falling to the floor. The whole barrage lasted a matter of seconds.

In the halted gunfire, Aram and Joachim heard the moans of the badly wounded survivor. They approached the three casualties and beheld the one still breathing. He was only a few years older than the two, but he had on a wedding ring.

"Give me the assault rifle, now," ordered Joachim, Aram quickly obliging. As Joachim aimed at the wounded soldier, the wounded man looked up with pleading eyes.

"Please," he said in a whispery—yet audible—voice. Both of his hands gripped the two biggest gushing wounds on his body. "Please . . . I have a family."

"Rodents have families," deadpanned Joachim before pulling the trigger of the assault rifle, pumping several more shots at close range into the soldier.

Scene 2

"How did you survive?" asked David Shapsdale to his guest, both in the study on that winter evening. He was still grappling with what Joachim al-Dunya had told him. "Why did you change?"

"Questions whose answers shall be revealed in due time," assured Joachim, standing proper by the small table with the firearm. Its muzzle still faced the host.

"Well," said an amazed David, letting out a brief laugh, "if anything calls for a drink, it is this little revelation."

The party host got up from his chair. Feeling a little tight around the body, he removed his jacket and draped it over the chair. Joachim offered no opposition to David walking over to the bottle with his glass. Once again, the bottle was tilted to the side and the contents poured into the broad bowl. He carefully placed the bottle back on top of the paper copy of the proposed legislation and walked back to his seat.

Joachim also took a seat, as though to console David at the news. "You have other queries?"

"Why a gun?" David pondered aloud. "You know me, Joachim. I have always kept a pill in my shirt pocket. I even replace it every year with a new one to avoid the risk of the potency being weakened with time."

"It is the appropriate punishment for you," answered Joachim, who maintained his straightened back and cool feel when seated. "You lived by the sword; now, you will die by it."

"Sounds biblical."

"It is."

David lowered his nose so that it was just above the brim of the glass. He inhaled the aroma of the red wine before taking a good swig of the contents. Placing the glass next to the gun, he grinned. "And you think that you can convince me to kill myself?"

"Well, the fundamentals are already present," began Joachim. "It is like the Old Testament. In it, one finds God walking amongst the earth, sin offerings requiring the spilling of blood, prophecies of a Messiah who will suffer, a virgin bearing a Child, and salvation being extended to the Gentiles. All that was missing was the Incarnation."

"An interesting theology lesson."

"You already have a willingness to commit suicide, as seen with that pill in your pocket. You already have a callous view toward life. And you already have so little to live for. You basically have nothing."

David looked around and laughed. "All these books and potables and I have nothing?"

"Merely a white-washed tomb," said Joachim dismissively. "You may have the trace of an existence—some disclaimer attached to a footnote marred by an asterisk—but nothing more. This window dressing is not a life. You have nothing."

"Then what do you define as something?"

"Something of lasting value. Like a lineage or a monument."

"You are correct, actually," David ceded. "I don't even have a homeland; I was never given a culture. You and I, Joachim, were set adrift like the rest of our race."

Joachim felt awkward yet accepting of the call to camaraderie in suffering. "Set adrift. Neither of us with basic things. No family."

"No family." David nodded.

"No buildings."

"No buildings."

"No homeland."

"No homeland. Permanent exile, no papers required," bemoaned David. "If either of us ever returned, their army would weed us out and deal with us harshly, hurling us into the greatest inevitability."

"And they would be justified."

"You say so. Wait a minute," said David, his eyes brightening. "I do have a legacy. I have the cause. And I have you." His confidence reemerged. His renewed cheerful demeanor caused Joachim to shift in his seat in discomfort. "You know, you were the most valiant soldier under my command. You really were, beyond all others."

"Even Aram?"

"Aram did things because he was told to. You did them because you believed in what we were fighting for. Loyalty—this was a trait that seems to have left you."

"You betrayed me, David. Not even just me, but everyone from the olden days," stated Joachim. "They drank of your maddening wine and listened to your poison."

"Now, now, Joachim, so cruel in your rhetoric," said David as he took another swig of the wine. It was like he gained strength from consuming the potent liquid. "When I came to Chaldea, I never expected to, fairly literally, run into a man like you—so yearning for knowledge, so willing to comprehend abstract concepts. And I keep asking how you survived, when it should be obvious."

"And now, I am here. We are here. It took me time, but it was accomplished. Sad to say, I had to use the very knowledge you taught me to track your whereabouts."

David smiled cruelly. "More than that; you are like a son, finding me, seeking me out like that prodigal of old. Indeed, when it all came down, I was hoping not only that you survived but that you also would go forth and continue the struggle."

"That was what you expected from your best soldier. I am the one that took your malice and made it mine. Your hatred became my hatred, and I fed off it and became addicted as you remain addicted."

"They say behavior is half-genetic," opined David, grinning once more as he saw the angered discomfort enter into the being of his guest.

"You are not my father," Joachim sternly said, leaning toward David, who leaned into the space between with a sparkly eye and cunning expression.

"I might as well have taken the title," said David, who leaned back into his seat while keeping the wine glass in his left hand. "You were fashioned in my image; I brought you up; and you learned so much from me. My best student, as well as my best soldier."

"I learned foolishness from you; I learned evil from you; and I learned how to do those horrible things from you. I was the student of a mad man—a spiteful man—and that man was you."

"Sad, sad is the day that I hear you speak those words, after all the good things you did for our cause," declared David, feigning a look of disappointment as he continued. "Do you really consider all those things foolishness?"

"Yes, for you ruined my life and the lives of thousands, if not tens of thousands of others. Those you claimed to protect, you either sent to the depths without a word of mourning or left them suspended in a living death, as you have me."

"I gave them a purpose, as I did you."

"You gave us nothing of value."

"Unbelievable," said David to himself as his guest became more and more visibly angered. "Joachim al-Dunya. My best soldier. The apple of my eye. A man who never strayed—"

"Shut up!" shouted Joachim, his right hand slamming the small table with a force that caused the firearm to hop a little into the air. Had the glass been placed on the surface rather than held by David, it likely would have tipped over. Joachim took a few deep breaths from his nostrils before calming down.

David had jumped back in his seat but kept his calm. His smile returned. "Now, now, Joachim. How can your little trial continue if I keep quiet about my crimes?"

"My apologies for the outburst," said Joachim, looking down. "You are correct in that utterance. You must detail your crimes this evening. What amazed me most about the others was that they really believed that by leaving the old country, they could escape the past. I proved them wrong. And I will prove you wrong soon enough."

David took another swig of the wine before gently placing the glass upon the small table. Even as he consumed more alcohol, his mood sobered.

Scene 3

Perziz Repha was in the bedroom at the motel in Chaldea. The humble dwelling was a major focal point for the eruption of violence throughout the occupied territories. While the funding and overall leadership came from Moab, the recruits and the coordination of detailed affairs came from those who gathered on that second-floor space. David Shapsdale was in the living room, reading a newspaper that Esther had been kind enough to give him. Neither of the roommates subscribed to any publications, not wanting to draw further attention toward their already notable activities.

Often, the two had visitors—contacts and agents of Moab. They discussed strategy, plotted attacks, and saw to getting more young men into the growing resistance movement. Masjids were a valuable help. None of the imams officially preached support for the guerillas to their congregations; however, some were known to pass the message along following prayers or at community gatherings. Since many of these clergy were related to individuals killed or driven from their homes in the last war, it was not a hard sell to get their help.

Repha was on the phone. Holding the receiver with one hand and dialing with the other, he made contact with the operator voice on the other end of the line.

"Yes, thank you, operator," said Perziz as he waited amidst the transitory silence on the line. With a familiar voice speaking on the other end, Perziz spoke up. "Hello, Vesuvius, I doubt much time has passed since we last talked . . . Well, well, I am happy to hear that you are doing fine . . . Vesuvius, have the reports come in . . . Is an eruption in the realm of feasibility?" Perziz went through his usual instant anxiety and relief at the query. His face went from serious to pleasant at the reply. "Good, good. I had hoped not . . . Pompeii is bustling, Vesuvius . . . Yes, exactly. Well, goodbye."

Perziz hung up the phone, again feeling better at the news. As violence escalated in the occupied territories, he assumed that the military would have uncovered their operation by this point.

An aid to this lack of discovery was that so many of the recruits were from the surrounding area, rather than concentrated exclusively in Chaldea. One village that provided a few dozen men was over fifty miles away. Their efforts to raise troops came with grassroots efforts, word of mouth, families talking to families, and—rarely—through official channels like press releases or website posts.

With his phone communication over, Perziz walked into the living room area where David was seated. Beside his newspaper was a glass of red wine, two-thirds empty. The opened paper obscured his face and upper body. Despite the shield, David was aware that Perziz had entered the room and the gist of what he had been doing.

"All is well, I assume?" inquired David, paper still hiding his face.

"Just fine, David," replied Perziz, evidently confident.

David read aloud from the news article: "'The triple homicide at the Al-Aziz Restaurant is the latest act of violence reported by Army High Command. Since the outbreak of guerilla war in the occupied provinces, officials have confirmed that forty men and women in uniform have been killed.'"

"And they say the media never reports good news," said a clearly satisfied Perziz. David, however, was more critical as he continued to read the article.

"'However, military sources also report astounding victories in defending outposts and bases against the guerilla fighters. According to military spokesperson Corporal Ruth Greenberg, 'Although exact numbers of enemy dead are uncertain given their policy of using explosives to cover their tracks, I would estimate that approximately three hundred guerillas have been confirmed as killed in action.'"

"What is the relevance, David? Those are the estimations of an enemy uncertain," countered Perziz.

David responded by reading once more, summing up the rest of the article aloud. "Morale among the people and the military is strong, and the prime minister has voiced his 'undying support' for the military operations in the region." David bent the paper forward so his angered countenance, complimented by forceful tone, appeared to his roommate. "Worse yet, I know for a fact *our* estimates state that more than six hundred have died; and at least another twelve hundred are wounded, captured, or have gone missing, likely to abandon our cause."

"Three hundred or six hundred, they were lives well spent for our race's liberation," stated Perziz, his smile no longer present.

"I am fast becoming disillusioned, Perziz," admitted David as he folded the paper and put it beside his wine glass.

"Do not become such," commanded Perziz. "We are making headlines—headlines both you and the rest of the world are reading."

"And the papers have portrayed us as sympathetic, right?"

"I sense your frustration, David, but consider the situation. They still have not found out that we are based in Chaldea. They keep running into other towns and villages, rounding up boys and men who they think are associated with us. It is only a matter of time before this gets out to the world as well."

"Is that going to be before or after we are massacred into submission by those pitiful children of rats and maggots?" asked David with great frustration.

"We can hold out; it is obvious," assured Perziz. "They cannot search every house and hut, lift every dress, and pull off every veil. This whole land cannot be subjugated, for they would have to cover it with a base at every few paces to do so. Chaldea has shown itself to be the best stronghold ever because it has a wall of ignorance protecting it."

"But we fight a losing battle. If we kill their troops, they only place more here. Parents gladly send their sons off to war—and their daughters, too," said David. "I warned you and the others about the dangers of doing this."

"Yours is still the job of getting more to volunteer for our side," reiterated Perziz, apparently trying to convince himself of their eventual success as much as he was trying to convince his company. "Resolve, David, resolve is the key to victory. If our resolve is greater, then we will prevail over those sub-humans."

"My resolve is waning," said David, sipping from his glass of wine. He rose and approached his co-conspirator. "I will confess that to you, Perziz. I have always wanted to fight a gentlemen's conflict over a gentlemen's disagreement; and now that I am doing so, my feelings that this duel favors against me increase."

"Guns are not an issue, and neither are bombs. All I need are enough young men to fight the war. That is all I ask, David Shapsdale."

"I give you that, my friend, I do. But they are catching on to our tactics."

"Then, change them!" declared Perziz, his own doubts in victory brimming to the surface where David could see them.

"How? They are figuring out everything we throw at them. Even most of the covert operations are beginning to have lists of dead and dying," said David as he paced back and forth. "We have set ourselves up for defeat; I can see this plainly. I mean, if Girgash were here, the first thing he would tell you—"

Then, David began to think of something new. His eyes went from looking at Perziz to staring into space. "Girgash . . . Girgash . . . " His face of worry transformed into a face of sadistic assurance. "Yes, I have it. Of course!"

"David? Are you all right?"

"Perziz Repha, my friend," said David. "I know how to do this. I know how to win this war. But I must tell Moab. He must give me approval and make sure everyone helps out. It is the only way."

"That sounds reasonable, I guess."

"Get in touch with Kadmon. Tell him I need to see Moab immediately."

"I will, David. If it is that important, I will."

"Good," said David, patting Perziz on the shoulder and then returning to his wine. He consumed the remainder readily as though he had already prevailed.

Scene 4

Kadmon welcomed David with the usual hospitality. It was the first time that the two had met in person since David was sent off. This was because David rarely left Chaldea, while Kadmon rarely left the villa and its surrounding area. Regardless, Kadmon treated him with much respect and directed David through the large compound to the very meeting room where he had first met Moab.

When he entered, Moab was found to be romancing one of the women who worked at his villa. It was nothing terribly graphic. They were seated next to each other, his arms around her. It may have been risqué for the region—however, within the walls of the villa, Moab reigned supreme. He and his female companion were not even stunned to have Kadmon and David walk in, as though no scandal were present.

"David," Moab kindly spoke, gently pushing the woman aside. "A pleasure to see you once again."

"Likewise, Moab," said David, standing before the seated man. Shapsdale decided to wear business casual for the meeting. At this point in his life, he rarely donned proper attire for occasions; but this felt too important.

"I am constantly amazed at your ability to recruit so many men to our cause. You must be quite the charismatic speaker."

"It helps when the audience agrees to the same intellectual assumptions," said David, with Moab nodding in agreement.

"I understand this is a matter of business."

"It is, good Moab."

The villa owner looked at his female companion and waved his hand; and with that signal, she nodded and quietly exited the room. Moab shifted in his seat, straightening up for the conversation to come. He looked at Kadmon, who nodded and proceeded to make sure the two men were given the utmost privacy.

With all save the two men absent from the chamber, David was beckoned to come closer by Moab. With a smile, Moab extended an open hand and pointed to a nearby chair.

David sat down.

"Tell me what is on your mind, David."

"It is the direction of our struggle, Moab. I fear that we are nearing absolute destruction. We are making no progress with the effort against the occupation. They are losing few, and we are losing many. They remain determined to stay and fight."

"Have you expressed these concerns to Perziz?"

"Yes, he is one of the few. I have been shrewd enough to deprive the underlings of such knowledge."

"Good," said Moab in relief. "I am glad to hear that."

"Good Moab, I have a new idea for how we can change our fortunes."

"I am listening," said Moab as he leaned toward David.

"It came to me the night before when I was lamenting to Perziz about what I thought was going to be our doom. I uttered Girgash Keniz's name in passing. And that was when I knew we could win the war."

"I do not follow, David. Educate me."

"It was how I killed Girgash and what I was able to do with his death. I got many recruits by lying to them about Girgash's demise. By saying that the military killed him, hundreds came to my ranks and, from them, hundreds more. By killing Girgash, I committed an act of atrocity. Murder, that is. I killed an unarmed civilian. Thus, I committed an atrocity and advanced false claims. These two horrid practices, violating two of the Ten Commandments, nevertheless led me to give our cause new life."

"What are you saying?"

"I am saying that if one instance of killing a civilian combined with one instance of advancing a false claim for a greater good can do this much, imagine the killing of many civilians and the promotion of many false claims. The trend will only be grander, the success only more total."

"David," said a visibly surprised Moab. "You come here to tell me that we need to engage in terrorism and propaganda to win this conflict?"

"Yes, I do," stated a determined David. "We must. We cannot cling to the dogmas of the quiet past to solve our stormy present, Moab. We must act like we are desperate; we must promote our message without regards to nitpicky facts. With these two methods, we will gain the world's sympathy and the world's support."

Moab was conflicted. He did not attempt a rebuttal of his younger peer's argument, nor did he wholly embrace it. Solemnly bowing his head, his fingers touched his temple as if he had a headache.

In front of him, David held his tongue, likely fearing that additional comments may ignite hostility. With a breath, Moab looked at his guest. David was fiery, undaunted, and passionate. Moab did not want to extinguish such an adamant sentiment, so he chose his words cautiously.

"Your conclusions are understandable. However, I have some reservations about this new approach you desire."

"Tell me them, good Moab. I can only benefit from feedback."

"I understand why you hate them. We all hate them. However, there are rules of war which—if nothing else—we need to adhere to in order to get the sympathy of the world. If we act as terrorists, the world press will portray us as terrorists."

"Not if we feed them the propaganda I want to feed them," quickly replied David, technically cutting off his host from speaking the next sentence. "We shall craft a modern blood libel, a narrative of genocidal cruelty. Whatever crimes they have committed, we will exaggerate them. Whatever things they may not have done wrong, we will spin them as wrong. I even have an example for you: I know that about six hundred guerillas have been killed. What we need to do is advance the idea that nearly six hundred *civilians* have been killed. After all, few, if any, of the recruits were actual soldiers in the literal sense. If we tell the world that the occupation has massacred hundreds of civilians within the first two months of this conflict, then they will listen. And they will be outraged."

"But, David," said Moab, "how would we get away with such a claim? By what means do we spread a lie faster than the truth can keep up?"

"The internet," stressed David. "The internet. That world wide web. I confess to not being that familiar with how it works. But if Perziz is to be believed, we can drop something on there; and large numbers of people will mindlessly promote it for us. It becomes 'common knowledge' within days, if not hours. As a result, it is not you or me saying that the military is slaughtering civilians wholesale—it is the average person."

"That could actually work," replied Moab, looking upwards in inspiration. "And it would take them a long time to learn it came from us."

"If they ever learn."

"Okay, that part makes sense," conceded Moab. "You have my blessing on that wing of your enterprise. It is the other wing that still concerns me."

"You mean terrorism?"

"Yes, I mean terrorism. Lying to people is one thing; violating well-documented conventions on rules of war is another."

"Now, now, good Moab," insisted David, "there was a time when neither they nor us bothered with rules of war. You remember those days better than I do."

"Yes, and I do not want them to return."

"But they must; they have to. We must make them tired of war, tired of wanting to resist. Then we have them—we have them to do with however we please. Have them fear us, have them long for a collective death rather than live beside us."

"Still," Moab insisted weakly, "it is hard for me to grasp the idea of killing unarmed civilians, women, and children. Even *their* women and children."

David thought a moment and then calmly responded to the concern. He put his left hand on the shoulder of Moab, prompting the host to look at the guest. "Think of it this way. They are all responsible. Their whole unrighteous nation is culpable in our suffering. The soldiers, we agree, are valid targets. But remember, there would not be soldiers if there had not been women to birth them. So, women are valid targets. The women became pregnant by the men of that country, who therefore aided in forming the soldiers. So the men are valid targets. The children either grow up to become soldiers or grow up to reproduce and generate new soldiers. So, the children are valid targets. The entire race that we fight is a valid target. They all are responsible for our suffering." David put his right hand on the other shoulder of Moab. "I ask you to give the order, to demand that the cause take these efforts. Chaldea, the headquarters, will lead the way. But a word from you, that will streamline it all."

"Your words are persuasive," stated Moab. "I will have to think on it. You may leave the villa at any time. This meeting is concluded."

"Yes, good Moab," said David, who let go of the shoulders and shook the hand of his gracious host. With a smile, he exited the room.

A moment after David left, Kadmon returned to the chamber. He waited for a few seconds before coming close to his boss.

"Moab? Are you all right?" inquired an unusually serious Kadmon. Moab looked up at his subordinate with unblinking eyes.

"They are all responsible. Every last one of them," said Moab.

SCENE 5

David Shapsdale and Joachim al-Dunya were many years younger when they walked down the main street of Chaldea that afternoon. Due to his growing youthful body and the passage of time, Joachim had recently passed David in height. David was in business casual, while Joachim wore a T-shirt and jeans. The town was mostly indoors, as many were attending social gatherings connected to the religious holiday. Those joining the two on the street were the poor and those giving them recently slaughtered animal meat. Prepared under Halal regulations, the servings derived from cows and goats.

"Things may seem tough, Joachim, but they are not lost," David confidently spoke as the two remained on the sidewalk. The poor and those aiding them did not pay the two any attention. "The military still has not found this place, and that is good."

"Yes, sir."

"As we get newer people to join our cause, I need leaders—people under me but still above those fresh bodies entering the fray," said David, who halted at the intersection. Joachim stopped in response. "I think you should be one of them."

Joachim was overwhelmed. "Really? You . . . you mean that?"

"Of course, I do, Joachim. When have I ever lied about such matters?"

"That's . . . that's great," stated the young man with a big smile. "I mean, I've never been in charge of anything. This will be so amazing. I barely deserve it."

"Well, it helps that so many people who were ahead of you are now dead."

"Yes, sir."

"And can you please stop calling me sir?" requested David. "I am not a knight."

"Yes, um, David."

"Actually, this reminds me," said David. "Joachim, how much do you know about knights?"

"A little."

"Knights were the ultimate Western soldier during the Middle Ages and so on, well before even I was born."

"Okay," said Joachim, attentively listening as another load of Halal meat entered the street to help feed the poor. Many indigents came from the surrounding area and not just from the least of the people of Chaldea. Most were hoping to be recruited into the guerilla forces that David and Perziz Repha were coordinating on behalf of Moab.

"The knights had a code, Joachim, of virtue and law that they imposed upon themselves. They would serve God above king, protect the virtue of women, abstain until marriage, rise up against the oppressed, and fight only those who could defend themselves. Things like that. This was the type of fighting force that once dominated the known world."

"Wow. They would be very helpful in this fight. I bet a whole detachment of knights should help turn the tide against the military."

"No, Joachim, they would not," said David, beckoning his younger company to follow him as they turned a corner. The street they entered was a minor road, which the town elders designated as one of the places where the animals could be ritually slaughtered. As a result, it had a disturbing appearance, with sheets of blood splattered all over the ground. Some of the butchers who did the work made bloody handprints on the building walls along the side, as a way of noting their deed. "In fact, to the contrary; having the knight present in this battle would be devastating for us and could possibly lead to failure."

"I'm not that stupid, David. I know that their technology couldn't compare to modern stuff. I mean that overall warrior class, David, that's all."

"No, Joachim, it goes beyond weapons," said David as they slowly walked along the side of the street that had few blood stains. A bunch of black-haired, barefoot little boys no older than ten took to cleaning up the layers of crimson. Each had a bucket and a mop, making slow but eventual progress. "For some time, their scruples could work effectively. But alas, our circumstances forbid such. Their code was called chivalry. That code—chivalry, that is—is an outdated mode of thought in the matter of war. We cannot expect to win if we use the code of chivalry."

"How come?" sincerely asked the impressionable youth.

"Joachim, we are at a disadvantage here. We do not have their capabilities. We have only minor explosives and guns, nothing more. They have helicopters, tanks, guns, manpower, and a strong determination. In order to counter that, we have no other option but to aim our efforts at their cities and homes."

Joachim was shocked. "Are you telling me that you want to attack women and children?" he asked in an outrage that briefly brought the attention of a couple of the boys, but only temporarily. The two stood in the middle of the back road.

David smiled at his young friend's concerns, dismissing them even before they manifested.

"They could barely be classified as being amongst such human types as women and children but what we have no other name for—yes, their women and children. It is necessary to turn the tide in our favor. I know that you are fretful."

"Yes, I'm fretful. I don't mind shooting a soldier or an officer; they can defend themselves. But women and children?"

"Aram has told me much about those successes you and he have in those ambushes. You are known for your appetite for violence."

"That's—" began Joachim, who knew David was correct. He conceded. "Yeah, I guess that is true, isn't it?"

"What makes it any less different to shoot a soldier who is already unarmed? Inform me of the disparities between shooting at close range a soldier who has dropped his gun and surrendered and the unarmed men who daily walk the streets of their cities."

"But still." The young man hesitated. "Still, they—"

"Are not human, Joachim. They barely have the ability to speak our language, if even having the brain capacity to form a government and manufacture guns. They are livestock—livestock waiting for the slaughterhouse. Not unlike the ones slaughtered earlier today. They are all responsible for our horrible situation."

"Why do you put the burden on me?"

"It shall not be on you alone, Joachim. It will be on all of us. The cause, the race. Everyone will respond to them in kind because all of them are responsible."

"But, sir—I mean, David—what about the others?"

"What about the others?"

"I am an imp at best, but the others are of practicing religion. Most I see darkening many a building of altar or prayer mat. How will they see this?"

David breathed an evidently annoyed breath but then lightened up and patted Joachim on the shoulder in assurance. "If they could compromise their beliefs enough to incorporate the importance of nationhood in a way of life that demands an end to jingoism, they will find a way to conform their values to this new strategy."

"I still doubt."

"In what manner?"

"I mean, okay," began Joachim, struggling to phrase his objections. "I guess, okay, well, I mean, let's say I agree to do this stuff. Which I will, of course. And then other people, like Aram, they agree to do this stuff. What about everyone else? I mean, I heard lots of other countries side with the military. They might see this as, you know, a good reason to—no offense, of course—hate us more. Or start hating us."

"I think I understand your concern," said David, left hand still on Joachim's shoulder. "However, I have already figured a way to convince the world of our righteousness. And you are looking at part of that process." David extended out his right arm and cast his hand over the sight of the boys cleaning up the animal blood. "Now, what I need you to do right now is to start taking photos of these kids."

"Why?"

"Because, Joachim, we want to win. And this is how we will win."

"With photos of kids?"

"With photos of kids cleaning up the spilled blood of their family members, all of whom were ruthlessly slaughtered by the occupation forces."

"But David, David," replied a stunned Joachim. "You and I both know that's animal blood from the Eid al-Adha sacrifices."

"Never let facts get in the way of a good argument. You and I both know that they regularly murder civilians. In fact, in the first two months of our uprising, those soldiers murdered over six hundred civilians. So granted, not factually accurate, but ultimately true. So here," ordered David as he took out a camera with film loaded. "Take some photos and let Perziz and me do the rest."

Joachim turned on the camera and held it up to his face to begin taking pictures. He paused and looked at David. "And this will help us win?"

"Yes," David firmly stated.

"Okay," said Joachim consenting fully to taking photos and taking lives.

SCENE 6

And it came to pass that the land was cast into darkness. The desert was known for its absorption of blood, the sands brushing away the carnages of the past. Not this time, not this era. People in both the proper country and the occupied regions were accustomed to news of violence. The past few months were noted for their dispatches from the front. Then came that one day, a day that was supposed to blur with the others in the minds of those who lived it—a normal, average day, meant to be one of a crowd.

Joachim and Aram got past the checkpoints without problem. They had done it before, setting up ways to get the necessary weaponry upon their entry into the enemy nation. Assault rifles in hand, they came across the normal community, passing through their pedestrian ways, automobiles starting and stopping at the lights. A nice, green square, a block to add nature to the material progress. Benches, a fountain, and plenty of foot traffic. The two went to different rooftops overlooking the green. Barriers at the manmade heights hid the two, both crouched with loaded weapons.

The rule was clear. Joachim was to fire first, followed by Aram.

Joachim steadied his glance through the scope. Studying the different people going about their routines, he spotted a pair of soldiers. They were casually strolling along the sidewalk, lightly chatting as their guns were slung to their backs. Unlike the many missions before, this militarized pair was not the intended target. Joachim moved the weapon so that the scope focused on some plainclothes adults walking by. There was no true aiming, no real focus on any individual. That was not the point. And so, without a firm centering on any person, merely the crowd, Joachim pressed the trigger and took someone down. Then another. Then another.

Aram followed suit, picking people off from the other building.

Screams, running, and people plunging to the ground. Cars stopped; police were called. Those with firearms of their own, soldier and civilian, attempted to shoot at the snipers. However, by that time, Aram and Joachim had vacated their spots on the roofs and had disappeared. The war had arrived.

David congratulated the two for their efforts, though he also expressed disappointment at the fairly low death toll. It was agreed that more suicidal acts were required to increase the rate of civilian dead. David made this charismatically plain when he spoke to the ummah gathered at the largest masjid in Chaldea.

Hundreds of young men heard his words, his appeal to the Jihad of the Sword, the need to kill even the women and children; for the whole nation was wicked and deserving of destruction. Soon they were arming themselves, submitting to the orders of David and others, like Perziz and Joachim.

Meanwhile, the buses continued to run through proper and occupied territory. One man, a teenager who had heard David speak, boarded a crowded vehicle. He paid the fare with paper money and coinage. As the doors closed and the vehicle slowly began to move to the next stop, he sat on the aisle side in the middle of the vehicle. A couple of the other passengers looked curiously at him, for he had opted to avoid taking a window seat nearer to the front. As the bus passed the twenty-five mile-per-hour mark, the teenager shouted a declaration of praise to Allah, tapped the center of his chest; and all was obliterated.

Corporal Ruth Greenberg's eyes widened when she got the phone call. The panicked voice on the other end could barely explain the event. Stoically replying that she was coming, she slammed down the receiver, forgetting to say her usual wish of peace. Private Shiri Dahan looked at her with innocent perplexity as Greenberg rose from her desk and ordered her to follow. By the time the two drove the jeep to the sight, firemen had already cooled the embers; and charred bodies were already lined along the street, white sheets placed over their remains. More were still being pulled out of the wreckage as Greenberg questioned the authorities present and Dahan questioned witnesses.

While David spoke to the masses in person, whipping the youths into a fury, Perziz was uploading photos and fables to the internet. Social media accounts across both the occupied regions and indeed the whole of the civilization became inflamed with the outrageous human rights violations committed by the military. Purportedly committed, that is. The cyber network spread the claims via email, links, message boards, blogs, and so much else. Frequently, all it took was to get to a few of the contributors to the body of online literature to spread it rapidly around the web, as thousands posted sans critical thinking. This, in turn, enraged more and provided increased support for their efforts.

That was how they were recruited, the three who got to the largest city in the proper territory. A metropolitan blending of cultures and races, it had a fashionable chic caste of citizens. They had their own restaurants, bars, nightclubs, libraries, book groups, and hangouts. One of these facilities, modeled after French cuisine, was having its usual bustling Friday evening business. Outside, every table had at least two people seated. Inside, over fifty mostly young adults partied and danced to the lights and music. It was a narrow building, placed between two other structures of broader scope. Still, it contained much room and atmosphere. Waiters and waitresses went into both areas, making sure every patron was having a good meal or a good time. That was normal.

Most looked in confusion at the three motorcycles that noisily pulled up to the main entrance. Some patrons were holding menus; others were drinking water or wine. At one table, a man was building up the courage to propose to his girlfriend. At another, an older couple was celebrating their fortieth anniversary. The bikers' faces were veiled by their helmets. Each one carried an Uzi, stolen from a weapons depot. Before any warning was shouted, two of the three opened fire, with casings and corpses falling to the ground. The trio then entered the vicinity of the outdoor tables, using pistols to finish off any moaning person. From there, they kicked down the door leading to the inside of the narrow restaurant, raised their Uzis, and fired nearly all their ammunition.

While David was integral to inspiring the youths to commit the final sacrifices and also plan overall attacks, it was Perziz who orchestrated many of the finer details. A frustrated soldier had recently opted to blow off steam by murdering a few villagers several miles north of Chaldea. Although the soldier had been arrested and was expecting to be tried soon, the resistance made sure that no one with access to the internet or to David believed that the system would convict him. With Moab's funding, Perziz was able to smuggle in the necessary supplies to make explosives. David convinced two men to make the one-way trip. The imams gave their blessing, and the white van left town.

The office building housed a thriving business. All twenty-five floors were dedicated to advancing the corporate interests in some way. The first floor included a well-managed daycare for the working parents. The third floor had an impressive food court with many genres of cuisine for the three square meals plus dessert. The top floors included executive board members, rising entrepreneurs, and other personnel. In a given work day, nearly two thousand people inhabited that homage to capitalism.

Its fatal flaw was that it was no more than three hundred feet away from the border between proper and occupied. Windows on the one side of the structure had a clear view of the checkpoint. It was a poorly guarded portal, since there was little traffic that came from the other side. Two guards and a simple barrier stood against a barren desert with one paved road leading to the metropolis. Since the vast majority of attacks had occurred north and south of their location, the military felt little need to expend more resources to protect that area; and the locals agreed. They felt safe. They always felt safe.

On that morning, a half hour before most of the staff planned to go on lunch break, a lone white van was approaching the checkpoint. It was not a strange thing to behold for the pair of guards. Such work vehicles periodically came and went for special deliveries or imports. When the guerillas had begun attacking military targets months earlier, checkpoint personnel adopted a stricter effort to search the cars before allowing them passage. They never found anything nefarious. Seeing this as routine, both men walked in front of the barrier, each with a hand up to remind the driver to stop.

But the white van only went faster, the growl of the engine heard by the two guards. The tires burned the pavement as they sped up. The two armed guards instinctively threw themselves away from the speeding van, which crashed through the barrier, smashing the wooden beams into splinters. The petty bulwark did little to slow their velocity, while the shots fired by the recovering guards into the back doors did nothing to hinder their advance. Praying to their god, the driver and his passenger readied for the eternal journey as the former turned the wheel to aim the automobile at the towering structure.

People heard the explosion from miles away. Numerous windows hundreds of feet from there were either cracked or shattered. Those nearby who lacked sight of the event thought it sounded like a lightning bolt striking close. Outside of the edifices of urban life—the restaurants, the office buildings, the hotels and motels, the schools, and so much else—citizens glanced outside their windows to behold clouds of dusts. Many assumed it was a sandstorm but then quickly learned that no such phenomenon was in the forecast. Then came the dread epiphany that the dust tempest was a manmade event.

The curious who ventured toward the epicenter of the clouds entered a growing vision of nightmarish inferno. Entering the clouds meant reduced vision, shades of brown obscuring the images common to city life. As the debris thickened, the landscape changed, with numerous small pieces of the glass-and-mortar building landing all over the streets, sidewalks, and roofs. The vast majority landed with little defacing, though as the people got closer, the falling debris became larger. Going deeper, windows of cars and structures were broken; walls were dented and scarred; and chunks of the road became unusable. Air became harder to breathe in as the particles thickened.

Closer and closer, whatever ponderings entered a traveler's mind were disrupted as emergency vehicles sped to and from the most wretched epicenter. Lights of yellow, red, and bright blue rapidly flashed on the tops and sides of the automobiles. Sirens of varying tempos were heard, each distinct mechanized creature offering a different service. It became more macabre as the tossed pieces were no longer just of the attacked structure but also of the people who once were there. Limbs, hands, sometimes only a finger, bloodied and dusted, scattered over the roads and rooftops.

Drawing within a hundred feet of the devastation, all trace of the sun was gone. The blue of the canopy was supplanted by the dark gray of the debris clouds mixed with the choking smoke from the many little fires that formed a loose confederation of conflagration. Beams and bricks, broken glass, furniture, cubicle walls, and corpses were strewn all over. The whole terrain had transformed into perdition. An army of public workers wore assorted uniforms from military to police to EMTs. They coughed and strained their eyes. Firemen were the best suited for the hellish conditions, with goggles and breathing masks that let them enter unto the depths of the monstrous ruins.

Police were the least equipped, though their primary purpose at this point was to look away from the nightmare and keep the routes open for any who needed to be evacuated to the nearest hospital. Frightened and weeping crowds gathered as the work continued— loved ones who demanded answers, curious citizens wanting to know what happened, and news media attempting to inform the world. Struggling to maintain their own composure, tough officers denied them entry to the realm of horror.

Few were recovered alive. The explosion and the collapse of the structure were total. Roaring fires were gradually subdued; local and national media outlets were allowed better access as the aerial particles became slightly less menacing. Broadcast journalists and their cameramen got closer, attempting to interview survivors, officers, and others. Most simply reported what they knew, with some of them having to cut their announcements short in their deep, overwhelming distress.

David Shapsdale was watching one of the outlets on his box television set in his motel room. He was not alone. Perziz Repha, Kadmon, Joachim, Aram, and a few others were there as well. There was gaiety and revelry among those gathered. Local wine was drunk; and fine meals, ordered from the best local restaurants, were consumed. David had a small TV dinner table on which he placed a glass of wine and a lush salad. A napkin tucked into his collar, he watched the violent images. Burned corpses being laid out along the way, crying relatives, emotional newscasters, exhausted aid workers, the overwhelmed and demoralized. As one newswoman provided the latest estimate death toll, he raised a glass to toast the news. That conniving smile came upon him, pleasure over what he saw and heard. A sip of the wine, he continued to watch the carnage inflicted upon flesh and metal, the outpouring of tragedy, all while casually eating lettuce, croutons, and dressing. Those with him were of a similar mind, boasting of their accomplishments, this by far their greatest. Their bragging got louder as the wine continued to pour. No clandestine festivity, a few of them talked freely to one another in the hallway, within earshot of a visibly troubled Esther.

As security tightened around the terrorscape, Corporal Ruth Greenberg and Private Shiri Dahan drove to the outskirts of the security points around the ruins. Their military IDs allowed them access to the destroyed structure. Greenberg clearly kept her feelings suppressed within, while Shiri struggled.

As they began to learn about what happened, Dahan looked over at the endless ruins. Something seemed to stick out of the grays and blacks of the wreckage. Curious and without speaking, she cautiously approached the little bright object. Kneeling down, she brushed away the soot and debris. At first, it looked like a wedding ring. Then, as she picked up the item with her hooked index finger, she saw that it was a dirty, light-green pacifier. Tears fell from her eyes as she covered her mouth with her free hand. Then, she went to both knees, bent over, and bitterly wept.

Scene 7

Press gathered at the military installation, where Corporal Ruth Greenberg and Private Shiri Dahan worked. There was a meeting room specifically designed to hold reporters and cameramen. Rows of armless chairs faced a platform that included flags on either side of the center. In the middle of the platform was a single podium with a microphone. Behind the last row of chairs was a cleared space that was filled with the legs of tripods and the cameras they supported. During times of relative peace, the place seldom had more than a few journalists. On that day, every chair was taken.

Corporal Greenberg was standing behind the podium, having just read a statement sent to her by high command. It was an update from the military as to the latest steps being undertaken to curb the wave of violence. She had read over the statement several times before entering the room. As a result, Greenberg spoke through the microphone with good projection and made frequent eye contact with the gaggle. Many were taking notes, preparing their probing queries for the spokesperson. After several minutes of speaking and the occasional flash from the photographers, the floor was open for individual questions. Hands were raised, as some spoke out to encourage being called upon. She saw one journalist in the second row from the front who had raised a hand early.

"Yes?" said Greenberg as she pointed to the reporter.

"Corporal Greenberg, what about the rumors some have that this insurgency is the product of the wealthy businessman Moab al-Aqsa?"

"Those are only rumors," stated Greenberg, knowing that undisclosed intelligence was indicating the same thing. "We cannot at this time confirm or deny them. Next?" Hands went up again, and some spoke up again. She searched for a few moments before locating the next journalist to call upon. After giving them a nod, the person spoke up.

"Some in the occupied territories are arguing that this is in response to the military's killing of Girgash Keniz. Is this the case; and if so, why did the military decide to take out Mr. Keniz?"

Greenberg did her best to hold back her annoyance. "As we have mentioned at other press conferences, there is no evidence suggesting that Girgash Keniz was killed by our military. An independent investigation confirmed that the bullet that killed him was not from a government-issued military-grade weapon. When attempting to establish blame, one must look toward the longstanding hatreds that have inhabited the region, which increased in ferocity when our country was founded. Next?"

The same practice as before, Greenberg found another reporter with a raised hand whom she cued for speaking up.

"Corporal Greenberg, um, I am curious as to whether or not you—or, for that matter, your superiors—are familiar with the recent statements released by assorted civil rights groups. As, um, you know, many NGOs have spoken out against the increased checkpoints and increased racial profiling in border towns. Um, how do you respond to their allegations that the military is engaging in, as they put it, 'gross violations of the rights and liberties of various minority communities'?"

"Let me stress that the military and the government and all good citizens of our country support civil rights. We respect the dignity of every human being and do our utmost to honor the rules of war. At the same time, our military is tasked with protecting our homeland, which has become more challenging, thanks to this recent terroristic phase of the insurgency. I assure you, whenever we look to improve our national security, we always do so with civil liberty concerns in mind."

"Liar! Liar!" screamed a young man at the very back of the room. He was by the main doorway, having just entered the enclosed space. His expression was of thorough rage. He had many photos with him, copies of the original.

Surprise came upon the gaggle, who directed their attention to the shouting figure behind them.

"That fascist pig is a liar! A bloodthirsty liar!"

Greenberg talked with a couple of the security nearest to her, her hand on the microphone.

Meanwhile, the man continued his tirade, passing out the photos. "Look at these photos! Look at them!"

Open-minded camera crew and reporters alike took hold of the graphic image.

"These poor boys are cleaning the blood of their family members. Families massacred by the military, by those pig-blooded Nazis! Two months! In two months, they murdered six thousand women and children! Thousands of helpless people slaughtered by those fascist pigs! End the occupation now! End it! End it!"

Greenberg called on security to remove the man as his ravings continued to garner attention and discomfort among the professionals gathered. Even as he continued to curse and spew allegations, the fourth estate turned away from the military spokesperson and began to consider what the activist was claiming. A few rushed out of the room to follow up with the man, consuming more of his claims.

Greenberg tried to sway them, assuring them that the interrupter's claims were unfounded. It seemed to work for some, but not for others. The ledes for many a story came from him rather than her.

After another half hour of questions that went without incident, Greenberg exited the room; and the gaggle went to their respective press rooms to run their stories. She walked down the corridor toward her office, having only a short amount of time to get some notes. Another round of being thrust into the media spotlight awaited her. On the evening schedule were a few one-on-one interviews with local media outlets. Her office door was ajar with the lights on. Upon opening it, she saw Shiri seated at her desk, pondering the recent events.

Greenberg's arrival seemed to do nothing to change her fellow officer's mood. Shiri was leaning back in her office chair, holding that light green pacifier she had recovered from the worst of the attacks. It was like she was in a trance, barely acknowledging her immediate company, much less the passage of time. Ruth neared her subordinate in pity.

"Are you all right?"

Shiri slowly looked away from the pacifier to see Greenberg standing before her. She resumed reverently looking at the pacifier as she spoke. "I do not know. When I first saw it . . . When I first saw ground zero of the attack, I cried. I cried a lot. Now, as I hear more and more news, more and more about the fullest extent of the tragedy, I can't cry anymore." She turned again to face Greenberg. "Have you ever felt so awful that you couldn't even cry? That is how low I feel. No release. No end. All night."

Ruth walked around to the side of Shiri's desk and leaned on it. She rubbed Shiri's shoulder before she spoke. "When my father fought in the old war, he used to keep it all to himself. He never talked about his experiences—all the awful stuff that happened. As he saw it, if he could just keep it over there, keep it on the battlefield, then he could leave it there when he got home and saw us. Even after I entered basic training, he rarely talked about it. I learned about most of his experiences from Ahmed—you know, the coroner you met? They served in the same unit, saw a lot of brutal action.

"The problem is, we cannot do what my father did. We cannot keep it over there because it is right here. It is in our cities and our streets. It is within our borders, next to us, coming among us to cause us as much harm as it can. We do not have the solace my father and Ahmed got to have. So . . . we will have to be better. We will have to be stronger than that generation. We must be better. And, you know—with God's help—we can be. It is just a matter of realizing what we can and cannot change.

"I do not know how long it will take for us to crush this insurgency. But I do know that it will eventually die. The forces of wickedness always eventually die. They always eventually lose in the end. We may not live to see it. We may only see the wicked prosper. But do not be deceived; they will fall."

Shiri seemed to be feeling better because of what she heard. Still clutching the pacifier with one hand, she turned toward her superior, visibly more optimistic. "Thanks, Corporal. I needed to hear that. I really, really needed to hear that."

"You know, if you need to," began Ruth, "you can always take the rest of the week off. Some new personnel are scheduled to be stationed here soon, and they could take over your work for the time being."

"No, no, that's okay," replied Shiri. "I think I would rather do something about this then sit it out, irregardless of how I feel."

"That is okay with me," said Ruth, who then looked down at her watch. "It's a little before 1700 hours, and I need to go to another site to do some interviews. I plan to leave for home from there. Be sure to turn everything off when you leave."

"Yes, Corporal," said Shiri with a weak smile.

After the two exchanged salutes, Greenberg gathered a few things and then exited the office, leaving the door about as open as it was before.

Shiri looked at the pacifier for a few more moments before gently placing it on her desk besides her computer. Also on her desk were files on identified insurgents, both those in prison and those at the morgue. A thought occurred to her, prompting her to go online to investigate some matters.

Scene 8

"What made you change?" asked David Shapsdale to Joachim al-Dunya, breaking a period of silence within the study.

"People change," Joachim answered flatly. "It was a surprise to me how much you have embraced the very upper crust life you once despised."

"A minor trapping," dismissed David, setting aside his wine glass on the small table. It was placed beside the firearm, which had yet to be touched since Joachim placed it there a couple of hours since. "Merely an alteration of costume. You, Joachim, are the one whose metamorphosis has been complete."

"You are correct; it has been thorough."

"So why the change? It is a ponderous contemplation. I couple it with the equally intriguing yet likewise unanswered question of how you survived."

"Which would you prefer an answer to?" asked Joachim, standing firm on the other side of the small table. "The question of plasticity or the question of endurance?"

"Plasticity," stated David. His dinner jacket remained draped over his chair, and his tie was loosened. The uppermost shirt button was unbuttoned.

By contrast, Joachim remained in proper form in his attire and, he mused, his mindset.

"Since you have chosen that question, I shall answer," said Joachim, after hesitating for a few moments to search his mind to effectively, carefully formulating the sequence of events. "The biggest reason for my turning away was the simple absence of you. No longer being constantly fed the deceptions; the fabrications; and the sly, convincing manipulation of your gifted tongue. Knowing as I already did that so much of it was hoax and falsehood, I simply concluded that ours was a cause that was fundamentally built on lies and wrongdoing. After everything fell apart, I went to the proper territories. I did not like it at first; but as time progressed, I came to accept them, to welcome them, and to acknowledge their basic humanity, cast in the image of God." He paced a bit as he continued, looking away for a time from his company, yet keeping sufficient attention to the firearm. "It was there that I heard the gospel preached. I learned that the Messiah had come for all lost sheep; that He showed no favoritism; and that all, Jew and Greek, are one in Jesus. These things led me to accept them—to accept their words and their presence in the land."

"You exchanged one brainwashing for another," accused David.

"Not at all," declared Joachim, returning to stand before the accused at his place by the small table. "My acceptance of them was built on the recognition that they, too, were imperfect. I did not assimilate every claim or accusation; after all, I learned from you that anyone can lie. I know of things they have done wrong, and I recognize certain valid critiques to their policies. But I realized that their fundamentals were valid; and thus, whatever their faults, they were the better side. I know I can do wrong. I know you can do wrong. You know I can do wrong. But do *you* know *you* can do wrong?"

David took hold of his wine glass by the stem and emptied its contents into his mouth. With an evidently unimpressed scowl, he talked as he rose to face the taller Joachim from across the small table. "Yes, Joachim, I know I can do wrong. I did it plenty of times. I surrendered to the necessity of barbarity ages ago. I did those things for the better good. Every suicide bomber I convinced to blow himself up in the name of Allah, I did for the better good. Every attack on civilians I helped plan, I did for the better good."

"'Why call me good?' asked the Lord to the rich young ruler,'" countered Joachim, citing Mark 10:18. "'Do you not know that only God is good?'"

"Spare me the righteous indignation, Joachim," began a visibly annoyed David, who took to pacing about his side of the small table. "You want a confession? A great and cathartic admonition of guilt? Fine! Here you have it. I did plenty of wrong. I lied so much that I made the very father of lies blush from the hallows of damnation eternal. So what? So what if I invented the occasional massacre? So what if I inflated the occasional statistic on civilian dead or took the occasional photo out of context? They still did wrong, wrongs that you in your moralistic slant deep down know to be wrong because sometimes they *did* commit massacres, especially in the earlier war. Sometimes they *did* wantonly murder us, deprive a village of water or electricity. Sometimes, it was by accident. Sometimes, it was intentional. So what? So what if one of their airstrikes hit the wrong house, killing dozens of civilians, by a sincere error? Lest I'm mistaken, the civilians are still dead."

Joachim pondered the defensive words uttered by the owner of the penthouse apartment. In his facial expressions, he put forth his own little hints of concession to the points made by David. Yet he was unfazed, and his mission was to continue. He expected these responses; he even welcomed them in his heart. "I am not here to paint them as infallible. I am here to note that none of these things would have come to pass if you and your lot had merely recognized their inherent God-given dignity and spent less time thinking of better ways to kill them and more time thinking of better ways to coexist."

"Look at what their occupation did to us, what it drove so many to do," David persisted. He was bent over, yet looking upward to his former lieutenant and current accuser. "Look at what they did to me. Look at what they did to you. Tell me they did not deserve at least some of the terror we gave them."

"I underestimated just how callous you can be, David," calmly spoke Joachim as he looked down at the weary company. "There is no justification for us. We were never justified. None of their acts were cruel enough, none of their injustices resounding enough. There were better ways; there were better options. There were plenty of venues we could have used within the system to correct any wrong. But we did not want to work within the system. Our bloodlust was far, far greater."

"Our situation was wretched. A tyrannized population has no better option than to water their fields with their enemy's blood."

"The Rev. Dr. Martin Luther King, Jr.; Archbishop Oscar Romero; Mahatma Gandhi; Jesus of Nazareth. They all peacefully resisted their oppressors."

"And all were killed."

"Yet their causes ultimately prevailed," passionately replied Joachim. "You, Moab, the others, myself—we could have been among their number. We chose terrorism instead."

David turned his back on Joachim and walked toward the other table. He took with his left hand the opened bottle of Chaldean wine and brought it to his glass. He filled the bowl about a third of the way up. The bottle was much lighter than before. Placing it back onto the other small table, where the printed bill remained, he silently returned to the place where Joachim was standing. Taking the glass by the stem, a thought came to him; and he placed the glass back down without touching the bulb to his lips.

"What if I was telling the truth?"

"We know you were not."

"Indulge me," David requested. "Entertain my little idea. For I am very, very curious."

"All right."

"What if I was telling the truth about them? What if they really had been trying to exterminate us? What if all the massacres and death tolls from their occupation were all accurate? What would you have done?"

Joachim breathed from his nostrils, not his mouth. Looking down momentarily before continuing, his gaze returned to David. "Well, if you were telling the truth about them—and there were no other venues for dissent or action of a peaceful nature—then the only option would be the route of armed resistance."

"Yes," said David, grinning in visible sadism.

"So, I would look toward organizing said resistance."

"Yes."

"I would recruit as many men as I could."

"Yes," said David, smiling a larger smile.

"I would look toward securing weapons and munitions."

"Yes," stated David more firmly, smiling even more so.

"I would train them, make sure they are competent soldiers who can strike at any time."

"Yes!" declared David, his left hand clenching into a fist of solidarity.

"And I would attack *armed* combatants, the soldiers who were committing the atrocities. I would fight a clean war." Joachim's last statement deflated all of David's enthusiasm.

The smile transformed into anger. Shaking his head in a display of absolute disgust, David walked away from his company, again turning his back. He laughed an annoyed laugh before responding, his head shaking some more.

"Oh Joachim, Joachim, Joachim," said David. "You are a putrid dreamer. Name one person from the old country who would draw such a stupid conclusion. Name one person who would agree with your idiocy!"

"Esther!" declared Joachim.

The very name caused David to shrink back and shutter as if a cold breeze had entered the study. His right hand gripped the shirt pocket that had the pill. After a few deep breaths, he let loose his grip and approached the small table. David looked down instead of at his guest, taking hold of the wine glass. He spun it around a few times, the red liquid tossing about the bowl like an ocean tide. Dipping his nose so that it was only a couple inches from the wine, he inhaled the aroma of the fermented contents before drinking it down to the dregs.

SCENE 9

Esther was not expecting to go on a date that evening. She wore no makeup and had her glasses on when looking at the night sky. It was after she had finished her shift at the inn and had eaten dinner with her father-in-law and his wife. As was her custom, she was alone. Esther did not want company at that point, yet she knew someone was coming. He was predictable in that way. Most nights, she welcomed his advances. His arrival amidst her controlled wonderment presented her with mixed sentiments.

"My stargazer out in the cold, isolated desert night. How goes it, then?" said a welcoming David, seemingly unaware of her internal strife.

"I am more or less the same," she replied, keeping her glance away from David, who stood behind her.

"A strange lack of emotion, this I can tell," said David, still smiling, yet evidently more cautious as he approached Esther.

"We have long talked of books and dreams, David, and what little reality spoken was so heart-wrenching that we again turned to the fantasy of literature as an escape."

"Where worlds can be made by man instead."

"Philosophy again," bemoaned Esther, trying to smile as David sat beside her. "I thought we had an understanding on how much I despise the practice in question."

"I know; I know," conceded David, briefly raising his hands as though trying to back off. "But you see, my business gives the audacity to oft seek converts to a tangible cause. To my memory, a good servant to my mind, you do prefer the tangible."

"I do, yes, I do. Again, I am brought to the realm of reality," responded Esther, her sea green eyes lowering to face the small desert ground separating her and her company. Her tone became all the more solemn. "I know what your business is, David."

"I would expect you to know by now."

"You sell death and destruction."

"For a noble cause," he defensively retorted.

"What noble cause demands the blood of children?" Esther inquired. "I thought that when the Christians came to this land and wiped out the pagans that child sacrifices had ended. You have proven the opposite."

David became angry. "I have proven that even the best men of history have to resort to evil deeds to advance victory. Your country is full of such examples. One of your presidents killed tens of thousands of civilians in one day."

"Those times were different."

"Planes bombed women and children constantly. But those pilots are hailed as heroes of the great arsenal of democracy."

"They were fighting a tyrannical superpower."

"So am I!" declared David. "That is what we are doing, Esther. Those inferiors are holding our entire race and our entire land hostage. They want to destroy my people."

"And what of me?" asked Esther, looking directly into David's eyes.

"What of you? You are not one of them."

"I am not one of you, either."

"You are different, though," insisted David, gently brushing his right hand against her left arm. "Esther, you are far superior to them. They are money-grubbing, greedy, debauched, and vain. If they had the chance—"

"They would say the same about you," interjected Esther, causing David to pull away in visible surprise. "Did you ever think that maybe your cause was wrong?"

"No, never," he responded; but she knew he once again spoke untruth.

"You point to my country for justification. We had a revolution once, centuries ago. We fought enemies that were intimidating. Our overseers were the greatest empire of that era. They had the best weaponry, the best discipline, and were well-fed while we had to fight on empty stomachs and—on more than one occasion—empty muskets."

"Yes, a harrowing tale," acknowledged David.

"But we never resorted to what you are doing. Even in our darkest hour, we never started to target civilians. We stayed on the straight and narrow; and we still won, even as the enemy themselves started to pull out all possible efforts to stop us."

"There were those who committed terror. I know that to be true."

"But they were not the norm. They were fringe and recognized as such."

"Regardless, we cannot win by using the quiet dogmas of the past. Look at what the military is doing to us. They are pulling out all possible methods and tactics: committing massacres in the hundreds, depriving towns of water to subjugate them, and violating the civil liberties of our race that live in their country."

"Those are lies. You know they are!"

"Most don't," stated David. "That is all that matters."

"Unfortunately, you are correct," said Esther. Her mood softened, her voice becoming tender once again. She was sorrowful, yet kept her state of bridled grace. She looked toward the stars before slowly turning to face David. "You have been a good friend to me. Every night we talk, I feel more human, more welcomed here. I feel pain when you leave because I know that it will be many hours before I see you again. How will I see you again if they come here and track you down?"

Before David was able to answer, music was heard in the background. The time of prayer had ended on that Friday evening; and the air, once filled with supplications and wailing calls, was consumed by boisterous melody. Usually, they danced, defying the conventions for unmarried men and women.

Esther drew back, her head bowed.

David seemed to understand the signal. Still, he leaned forward and kissed her on the forehead.

Esther made little external reaction, as she had been kissed plenty of times in her native land. Internally, she was flushed with many conflicting emotions.

David got up, dusted off his pants, and walked back to Chaldea.

Minutes later, Esther did the same.

SCENE 10

Corporal Ruth Greenberg was able to get through the interviews without incident. She ate her dinner alone at her apartment that evening; she had had enough public attention. The following morning, she went through her usual routine. As always, this resulted in arriving at the military installation several minutes before her official clock-in time. Banal pleasantries were exchanged with the receptionist. More basic greetings were exchanged with some of the other personnel that worked in other offices.

Walking down the hallway, she saw her door was still open and the lights on. Her initial reaction was annoyance. Apparently, Private Shiri Dahan had forgotten yet again to close things down before leaving. Her subordinate's absent-mindedness was sparse but documented. Pushing the office door fully open, Greenberg discovered that the real reason the lights were on and door ajar was because Shiri had not left. Rather, she was still in her seat. Slumped over on her desk, unconscious, but still in uniform.

After Greenberg put her things on her desk, she walked over to where Shiri was seated. As she got closer, she was better able to see the sleeping soldier past the bulky, beige computer monitor. The button for the computer unit was a flickering orange, implying that the machine had not yet been shut down. Shiri's beret was placed on top of some files stacked on one side of the computer. Her hair was freed from its standard ponytail. The keyboard was pushed back to give her upper body room to lay on the desktop without imprinting small squares on her face. To her right was the light green pacifier.

Neither the overhead lights nor the entering of her superior woke her. Shiri breathed peacefully in rest, the faint inhale and exhale being the best evidence that she was still alive.

Greenberg thought a moment on how best to disturb the serenity. She opted for the same approached that her former superior used to do to her whenever she was found asleep. The corporal fashioned her hands flat as though about to clap them in applause. Rather than do so, she located an empty part of the crowded desk and slammed her two palms onto the desktop surface, immediately waking Shiri.

Shiri shot up in a panic, breathing rapidly from the sudden return to consciousness. After looking around wildly, she saw that the source of her alarm was standing in front of her. Seeming to be intimidated, Shiri quickly rose from her chair, pushing the wheeled furniture back a few feet when she got up. While still at attention, she saluted, her breaths continuing a rapid pace. After the salute was accepted, she went about fixing her hair back into a ponytail and grabbing her beret. "I am very sorry, Corporal. I must have fallen asleep while working."

"They shoot soldiers for doing that," Greenberg coldly stated.

"But I was not on the clock. This is not a post . . . I mean . . . I mean, what time is it, anyway?" asked Shiri, her eyes showing strain even with the few hours of break from screen time.

"It's 0840 hours," said Greenberg.

"Oh, okay," said Shiri, smiling in visible relief. "Then I still have another twenty minutes before I would be literally committing a shootable offense."

The smile was not reciprocated. "Get some coffee," ordered Greenberg as she retained a proper formality about her physical and mental presence. "It's going to be another long day."

"Oh, that is why I am here," said Shiri, showcasing bewildered excitement. "I think I found out where the insurgency is based."

Greenberg was unimpressed. "We know that already. The occupied territories. Now, like I said, get some coffee."

"Yeah, I know. But I mean . . . I mean, the center of it all. Where's the power coming from? It's not as random as you think."

"You mean Moab?"

"Maybe him. Most likely him."

"We have covered this matter with intelligence," reminded Greenberg, who was about to turn away to get to her desk. "While we are sure he is behind it, we have yet to find a link."

"Well, I think I found the link. At least, I mean, that is, where all the guerillas are being recruited and trained. The specific place."

Greenberg ceased her motion and centered on Shiri. The corporal remained formal though with a strained patience. "You have my attention, Private Dahan."

"Well, okay, good," said Shiri, evidently trying to compose herself. "Um, well, first of all, I need to get my computer running." The private took hold of the mouse and moved it around a lot in the hopes of getting the machine's attention. With a couple of "come on, come on" statements, the computer finally awoke and showed her the screen with icons. She conducted a quick search and found the correct icon.

Moments after clicking it, a map appeared on the computer screen. It had a large gathering of random green dots.

Greenberg changed her position to better view the monitor.

"This, as you know, is a map of the occupied provinces. Each of these dots represents the hometown of one of the identified terrorists. As you can see, no real pattern found here."

"I really hope you did not spend all night working on a map that tells us nothing," critiqued Greenberg.

"Oh, no, not at all, not at all," assured Shiri, who clicked on the document's upper righthand corner to minimize it. "I will show you what I found, but first I have to tell you how it literally came to me. Anyway, I realized that there was no pattern just when focusing on hometowns. But then it occurred to me. People have other links to other places. Totally common. I mean, I'm surprised I didn't think of it earlier. Anyway, so I decided to go online and see what I could find on these terrorists on social media."

Greenberg opened her mouth in anger, ready to berate her subordinate about how she felt about people using the office's computers in such a way.

Shiri interjected before the words could be uttered. "Look, look, I know that you don't like it when I go on social media at the office; but let me tell you, it was a gold mine. A real gold mine. People put *everything* on those sites—where they work, where they went to have dinner, photos of parties, all sorts of stuff.

"So I started to look at all the posts and accounts that these guys had, and I found tons of info. I looked at things like where they went on the weekends and where some of them worshipped if they didn't worship at their local mosque or church. I looked at sources of employment, stuff like that. And, I mean, things started to come together. I went back to the map and reworked it based on what was coming up. And here is what I got."

Shiri searched for the document on the screen as an interested Greenberg got closer to the monitor, standing behind and over the private. Shiri clicked on the document; and after a few seconds, another map of the occupied territories popped up. This time, however, the dots were blue, and they showed a very clear pattern.

Greenberg was thoroughly surprised.

"As you can see, Corporal, when factoring in any connections, about two-thirds of them have a relation to that specific town," said Shiri as she pointed at a small part of the map, her index finger nearly touching the screen.

Her superior was still skeptical. "Private Dahan, you mentioned that this might also link to Moab. How so?"

"Well, it was a challenge at first," admitted Shiri, as she looked away from the computer screen and stood beside her superior, her hands moving as she talked. "After all, we have yet to see him go there in recent years; and intelligence never found any business ties or things like that. I mean, he is largely disconnected. But—but I did look at his known acquaintances. Apparently, one of Moab's, shall I say, 'lady friends' was born and raised there. So he's not totally disconnected. You see?"

Greenberg folded her arms. Shiri was losing some confidence, but kept at it.

"I think we need to get a force assembled—some armor and some planes—and we need to take that place out," insisted the private.

Greenberg remained silent for a time. Shiri was doubting whether or not she had made her point with total effectiveness. After a period of time that felt far longer for Shiri than it actually was, the corporal spoke up.

"Let me see if I have understood you correctly, Private Dahan. You want to launch an attack on a small, isolated vineyard town because a heap of circumstantial evidence based on loose connections garnered from social media indicates that there might be a terrorist organization at work in said town. You want to risk the entire reputation of the military based upon a very fragile link between our enemies and a village in the middle of nowhere. How do you know that all of this is not merely a bunch of random coincidences?"

"Well, as a wise person once told me, 'Just because there's a God in Heaven doesn't mean there isn't a devil in Hell.'" Shiri smiled nervously after quoting her superior.

Ruth faintly nodded and then even gave a wry smile at the response.

At that moment, Shiri knew she had won.

ACT IV

Scene 1

Perziz Repha was finishing up some matters on the computer when David Shapsdale entered the apartment at the inn. Repha was updating the website and social media pages for the cause, as well as messaging new propaganda for the many blogs he kept in touch with. The rapid spread of their claims was only proliferating. Indeed, efforts had even entered the entertainment industry, as many television programs were referencing the conflict from the insurgency's perspective and at least one film was released to rave reviews. Perziz wanted to inform David of the developments, but the man entered the place in low spirits. With little spoken, David went over to his bed and laid down, eyes open, staring at the ceiling.

Perziz exited out of the webpage and continued with his other important task. Walking over to the mantle where the landline phone was located, Perziz picked up the receiver and dialed for the operator. Following the usual exchange, customary at this point, Perziz was directed to the source he had interacted with since day one of the operation. After three rings, a voice was heard on the other end. And the disguised communication began between the two people, at first in the typical fashion.

"Yes, Vesuvius, all is going well here," Perziz noted aloud as he sat on his bed, looking away from David. "The other villages are still sending help. So then, what of the volcano?" Perziz paused to hear the response. Upon getting the news, his face twisted to a fearful expression that bordered on the comedic.

"There is an expected eruption?" he nearly shouted, drawing the curious attention of David. "How severe, Vesuvius . . . *Total?* . . . That sounds horrible...Oh, no, no, do not fret, Vesuvius . . . Pompeii will organize the evacuation as soon as possible. Thank you for the warning, goodbye!"

"Eruption?" inquired David as he got to a sitting position on the side of his bed. David beheld Perziz as he took his backpack, laid it on his bed, zipped it open, and began to fill it with various things.

"Yes, David Shapsdale, an eruption. Vesuvius is going to erupt," said Perziz, who then paused to think. "Wait, why am I talking code to you? The army finally figured out where we are based, and they are coming this way. My source expects them to get here no later than early morning."

"You mean that—"

"They are coming for us! We need to evacuate, to leave, *now*, David," urged Perziz, who finished tossing most of his clothes into the backpack. He then made his way to the computer, where he took all the floppy disks and a new flash drive—along with printed notes and information—and tossed them all into the opened pack.

David got up, seeming to be hesitant to speak as his companion continued to get ready. "I understand what you are saying, but I still disagree."

"What?" asked Perziz, his packing halted.

"We cannot just leave. These people—they have given us room and board; they have given their lives for this. Now, at the darkest time of their need, we retreat and leave them to some horde?"

"Yes, we do, David. You said it yourself way back when: Chaldea is a vulnerable area. It would take them less than a day to surround us. Within an afternoon, we would have to lay down our arms," said Perziz. "Those were your words, by the way."

"Still"—David defiantly stated—"I will not leave."

"Are you stupid?" declared Perziz with both arms raised. He quickly realized the situation. "No, you're not stupid; you're worse than stupid—you're in love!"

"I will not waste the air and tell a lie," spoke David. "Her name is Esther."

"I know who Esther is," said Perziz, who went into the bathroom to get his toiletries, quickly reentering the bedroom and tossing them into the opened backpack. "She took our money and your heart."

"And I hers."

"We have to leave tonight, David. Even as we banter, the army gets only closer. They have infantry, tanks . . . you name it. They are going to level Chaldea to the ground. Total destruction is expected. It will be like the days of the Old Testament."

"I cannot leave without Esther; I just cannot," insisted David.

Perziz thought for a moment as he zipped his backpack closed. "Then, take her with us. It would make the desert journey harder, I know. The rations would have to be stretched a little; but we could make it, make it all the way back to Moab."

"Cannot be done," countered David. "Come on, Perziz, you know the customs in this town. Esther is forbidden to travel with men who are unmarried or unrelated."

"Then, marry her! You said it yourself that you wanted to leave the ranks of bachelorhood."

"Her father-in-law, who is her legal keeper, does not yet know of me. Further, he is more traditional-minded and would want a planned wedding. Esther told me herself. I am staying," replied David. "Why don't you?"

"I have not fallen in love."

"Beyond that, Perziz, beyond that. You would sacrifice these people that quickly?"

"I would, and I will."

"That is insane and counterproductive."

"Did you learn nothing of Girgash—how you had to kill him in cold blood to survive? Such is our situation, David. Except this time, Girgash is supplanted by Chaldea; and the pistol has become the army."

"We could fight and still give them losses. There is a chance, given their strong value for human life, that we could win."

"You dream too beautifully."

"Still, at least plant your sword and standard into the ground, destined to be bright red and fight alongside me and the others. Why do you betray your race, Perziz?"

Perziz gave David a gaze of sedated anger. Perziz walked up to him and in a calm, dark tone explained his reasoning: "You ask why I betray my race, and I tell you that you ask the wrong question. I have not—nor will I ever—betray my race. Unlike you, David, I realize that this goes beyond this place. By killing those depraved imperialists, we are doing the world a favor. That subhuman clan has plagued the whole human race for millennia. From the onset, they have corrupted every civilization they have touched, turning the people into money-grubbing, foul-bred ingrates who do not know right from wrong. If sacrificing this town will give us an extra step in destroying them, then so be it."

David evidently found little to disagree with in the words of Perziz. Nevertheless, it was clear he was not going to accompany him through the desert that night. "I stand where I stand, Perziz. I just ask that we end on good terms."

David offered his hand, which Perziz shook.

"In all of this, you became a good friend. I will never forget that."

"And my ranks salute you, for they would not be as thick and well-stocked had it not been for your golden throat and silver tongue. To say nothing of the sound intellect and mental domination. As I leave, and until the greatest inevitability hits me, I shall not forget your service to the race," said Perziz in sincerity.

He took upon himself the heavily laden backpack and was about to exit the bedroom. Then, something occurred to him; and he stopped. Perziz removed the pack and returned it to his bed.

David briefly wondered if his words had convinced a change of heart on the part of ally, though he quickly knew better and dismissed the notion.

Perziz unzipped one of the compartments of his backpack; and he took out a pistol, the very same firearm David had used to murder Girgash Keniz.

"I think you might need this more than me," said Perziz as he handed David the weapon.

"Truly," he replied as Perziz again strapped the backpack onto himself. "Salaam."

"Salaam," said Perziz as he exited the bedroom; and then the unit; and, from there, the inn; and then, finally, Chaldea.

David looked at the firearm, coddled in his two hands. He then let it be held by his left hand alone. Stretching out his arm, he pointed it forward, aiming at nothing in particular. Lowering the weapon, he sat back down onto his bed. He knew that much would have to be done that evening in preparation for the following morning. Looking at the handgun once more, he took a deep breath and pondered the obvious murmurs aloud: "How in the blue blazes did I get myself into this one?"

Scene 2

David Shapsdale and Joachim al-Dunya were sitting silently in the study at the former's penthouse apartment. They were on opposite sides of the small table that had the handgun laid upon its top. The silence had extended to nearly two minutes. Joachim stared at the party host, his eyes unnerving to behold. He was patient, but he was determined. David was thinking, his wheels turning rapidly yet recklessly. His mentality was losing its inhibition. He grinned near the end of the pause and spoke up.

"Are you familiar with the works of Francois-Marie Arouet de Voltaire?"

"Not as well as you, I assume."

"He is one of my favorites. He once said, 'They that can make you believe absurdities can make you commit atrocities.'"

"I assume this route has a particular destination."

"It does, indeed," assured David as he rose from his chair, which had his dinner jacket draped on the back and the tie slung over the top. "You know, I have always found it funny those war trials of those officers, the ones who were part of the fallen tyrannical regimes. Do you know what they always say without fail when they are caught?"

"You would know."

"'I was just following orders,'" deadpanned David. He then became more mockingly exasperated in his tone. "'I was just following orders!' They always shift the blame from themselves to someone else." Then, entered more sarcasm. "'We couldn't help it; it wasn't our fault.'" The impersonation ended. "Convenient, is it not?"

"What is your point amidst that heavy amount of words?"

"My point is this, Joachim al-Dunya," began David, pointing at his seated guest. "You are the same as them." He then erratically paced back and forth, his movement stopped and voice raised at certain times to make his points. "You preach to me about how horrible I am, how awful a human being I am. I am blameless, Joachim, blameless! Outside of Girgash, I have killed no man. On the other hand, you— yes, you!—have killed many men . . . and women . . . and children. Say it, Joachim! 'I was just following orders!'"

"You were behind the whole of the crimes committed," declared Joachim.

"Me? Little, old, gentle me?" playfully responded David. Again, he pointed in indictment toward his company. "Who was the one who pulled the trigger that ended many a life? Who was the man who actually stared into the eyes of those precious little children and shot them dead? Who was the one who planted the bombs, depressed the buttons, and celebrated the cause by launching rockets and mortars?"

"You lied to us," angrily replied Joachim. "Your promises were numerous that the terror was a temporary action, a minor means of holding them until proper munitions were supplied. You said it was for a just cause. You said this and more."

"And you had the idiocy to believe me!" shouted David, his voice raised higher than at any point in that evening so far. "It is amazing that you, the 'holier than thou' man with the gun and purpose in tow, can complain about anything. If you are blameless, Joachim, then how come you so easily fell in step with the others, huh? You were such a flunky—a flunky like the rest of them. You, Aram, and the others became nothing more than an extension of myself. You were another arm, another leg, another hand."

"You did deceive many."

"I did not deceive; I had a message. Could I help it if so many believed it so thoroughly? You are included in that number. Either you were so idiotic back then that you barely realized just how much of your humanity I took away from you . . . or you were willing."

"I was willing, back then," admitted Joachim with an expression of true shame.

"Yes, you were very willing," said David, smile emerging. "And I will say, I do not blame you. Our mutual loss of good morality was understandable considering who we were up against." David shed the layers of sophistication as he continued, reaching into a sense of guttural rage. "That horrible, disgusting people, if even the word 'people' could be ever allotted to them. You had no problem with destroying that mud wallow of a race, and nor do I. Those pig-bloods, who are nothing more than a race of maggots and leaches, who pin themselves to the healthy human body and suck it dry of its purity. Those colonialist pigs, those slime of wallows, those Christ-killers, those vampires of the nations!"

David stopped his words, breathing heavily. The energy of the vitriol, combined with the dialogue and debate from the past few hours, drained him. Yet also was the shock, the amazement David had for his openly expressed contempt. Amazed he was at being capable of such rhetoric after years of refraining.

"The passing of time is such a powerful weapon against man," observed Joachim, remaining seated. "Empires of strength and power fall, leaving mere trace evidence of their luster. The pyramids rise from the desert landscape only to be gradually eroded and swallowed back into the arid sea. The ways of the wicked prosper for only a while, and then they, too, collapse and are buried."

Joachim stared at the host with unflinching resolve. "I am getting to you, David Shapsdale. In all the time I have known you, your voice has never been raised so high and in such hateful agitation. Whether you like it or not, you will die before the sun rises, before it again warms the city that hides us now."

"The greatest inevitability," said David.

"No, it is not," responded Joachim.

David became aggravated. "You know, Joachim, you keep saying that over and over. At every point it seems, I mention my prized description of what all flesh is destined for; and then you dissent. Are you a ghost? Are you immortal? Such critiquing is beyond my shallow will and gets ever more embedded into my cherished ire. For what, oh what, good Joachim, what in all the universe, what in all creation, is more inevitable than death?"

"You will find out soon enough," assured Joachim.

SCENE 3

Chaldea awoke early that day, pulsing with activity in the hours leading to the dawn. Young men armed for battle; plans were discussed and coordinated among David Shapsdale's lieutenants; and others went to cellars for succor. The streets were vacant by the breaking of day, as few wanted to be seen by any planes that might fly overhead. David and Joachim were among those making rounds from building to building, hiding place to hiding place. Even the beggars were taken in, offered assault rifles and a quick training session on how to use the rapid fire weapon. Most shopkeepers and elderly, those who could not or would not fight, lent themselves to serve as medical help.

At one of the schools, thirty boys were standing in three lines of ten. They ranged in age from twelve to four. Most were tanned, the rest pale. Two had light brown hair; one was blond; and the rest had dark or black follicles. They wore bland clothing, T-shirts, and jeans. A few had tennis shoes, but the rest were barefoot or sandal-bound. Each one wore a vest, and each paid the utmost attention to the bearded, bespectacled imam who spoke with them. He was the oldest adult in the room. Several others were there also—a few mothers, one father, and a few younger men who were technologically literate.

"Each of you is a warrior for Allah," stated the gray-haired imam, with most of the adults nodding in agreement at his words. "You are here to fight the infidel, to drive him from this land. The infidel struck first. He came to our land before you were born and assaulted the ummah. Now, dear warriors, you will strike back."

The imam then spoke about the vests each boy was wearing. They were khaki-colored and dangerous. "The way you shall enter Heaven is through the vests you now wear. All of you must go to the nearest infidel and be sure to blow yourself up, sending them to Iblis and yourself to Paradise. For you older children, you will be responsible for pushing your own button. It is located at the center of the vest. For you younger warriors, we will handle the trigger. We have a couple of fine devout Muslim men who will witness how close you get and, when the time comes, will remote activate your vest, thereby sending you to Allah. Now, any questions?"

"Is there chocolate in Heaven?" asked a bright-eyed five-year-old in the front row.

The adults displayed a varying array of emotions at the question. Some of the other kids looked at the little boy, the older ones rolling their eyes. The imam approached the child, bent over, and responded with a grandfatherly tone.

"More chocolate than you can ever imagine," he assured the youth, who smiled at the thought of limitless carnal pleasure.

A few blocks away, Aram and Joachim were waiting with dozens of others inside the hookah bar where they first met with David and

Perziz. It had been a couple of years since they talked about taking part in a resistance movement. The hookah stands were removed; and every person within the establishment was young, male, and armed. Most had Kalashnikovs, as well as the occasional pistol and several grenades. Missiles were located elsewhere in the occupied territories and were reserved for cross-border attacks.

Aram watched outside, waiting intensely for the enemy to appear.

"Hey, Aram," said Joachim, breaking his friend's steely concentration.

"Oh, hey, Jo."

"You all right?"

"It's happening. It's finally happening."

"I know. Crazy."

"I got to admit," began Aram. "It's going to feel weird shooting at soldiers. I mean, I did it before; but it's been a while."

"I'm sure you'll do just fine."

"I hate them," stated Aram. "I hate all of them."

"So do I."

"I hate them more."

"It's not a contest, Aram."

"I want you to know, you've been good to me," said Aram, hesitating before he continued. "And I had a blast knowing you. I hope that whatever deity rules the universe lets us meet again in the next life."

"Aram," said Joachim in a worried voice. "What are you getting at?"

"I hate them so much. I cannot live in the same world as them. I don't care anymore. When they breathe our oxygen, I feel poisoned."

"I asked you a question."

"When they show up, no matter what, I will kill them," declared Aram, pulling back his jacket to reveal a khaki vest much like the ones the kids were wearing. "And if that means I got to go, then so much the better."

"Aram!"

"I got to do this, Jo," stressed Aram. "It will feel so much better than living with them. There is nothing you can say to stop me. We're all going to die, anyway. As David always says, it's the greatest inevitability."

"Maybe it is," said Joachim. "Just be ready to take it off when we win."

"You got it," agreed Aram.

Joachim patted him on the shoulder and then exited the hookah bar, going to a few other places to check on guerillas before selecting his own spot for the forthcoming onslaught.

The inn where David and Perziz rented a room was almost empty. David had told Esther he was unsure how much the military knew about their positions. He therefore feared that they might know the exact building where they were concentrated. If so, they might launch an air strike to level the structure. David had decided to have as few people at the motel as possible. One of the few still there were Esther and her father-in-law, who was seriously ill and had sent away the rest of the family, yet for some reason failed to include Esther among the evacuees.

Esther was unsurprised to learn she had been overlooked. She stood loyally at her post, waiting behind the front desk in the lobby. To pass the time, she examined and re-examined the business books. Esther looked up with her glasses on when David entered the room. He had patches under his eyes, apparently having gotten little sleep since the night before. It was still early morning; and she could tell he must be tired from going all over the town, relying only on adrenaline and anxiety to keep him awake. Esther paused when she saw him.

He silently and slowly walked from the entrance to the desk. A faint smile came upon his face as he stopped in front of the desk, leaning his hands against the desktop.

"Good morning," he said, seeming to knowing nothing better to say.

"Good morning," replied Esther, likewise unaware of a more suitable response.

"I just wanted to say," David said, then hesitated. "I wanted—*I want* to tell you." He laughed at himself. "You know, I have no idea what I want to tell you. That is how awful I am right now."

"It is an awful time," agreed Esther, looking down at the desktop. "My father-in-law is too sick to travel. I must stay here and watch everything be destroyed." She looked up and queried without hostility. "Why do you come here? Why are you seeing me now?"

"I just had to," replied David. "I need to. The very thought of you not being in my life frightens me. It scares me more than anything coming our way. Am I afraid to say that I love you? I have said it before. But now, now when it feels the truest, I am the most terrified."

"My father-in-law should be safe," she said, again looking down. "He is in the cellar. He is elderly and unarmed. They should spare him."

"Most likely," admitted David.

She looked up again, her sea green eyes captivating the weary man. "When it is destroyed, when it all falls apart, we must be together. We can run away. We can escape this butchered world. I want you, David. I want a future with you. Is there any way you can tell them to surrender? The children, at least?"

David shook his head.

"Then, the monster has become more powerful than its creator."

"It has."

"Who will you love more?" asked Esther as her eyes pierced David's. "Will you love this cause, or will you love me? Because I do not know which thought hurts more: me living without you, or me living with your hatred."

"Why must you make me choose, Esther?"

"Because I hope that you are better than what you do to those you hate. If it is not so, then I do not know what I can do next."

Before David was able to give an answer, a noise went through the silent town. A rummaging, droning noise. It was the sound of many motors, of many tires and tire tracks. They were nearing.

David gave Esther a kiss on the cheek. He evidently did not want to leave, but the sounds were getting louder. They were almost in Chaldea, and he had to be elsewhere. David backed away, then turned to run out of the entrance.

Upon his disappearance, Esther felt a great, piercing pain within her heart.

David avoided detection from the military. He was within a separate facility as the tanks and troop transports crawled onto main street.

Trucks with covered backs unloaded the soldiers. Men and women, representing diverse shades, faiths, and ethnicities—some even brethren to those within Chaldea—flooded into the streets. They wore shades of tan that mostly blended with the desert background.

Body armor, helmets, and assault rifles with scopes were common. They cautiously went up and down many of the byways, seeing no sources of alarm.

David was effective in hiding the guerillas.

Minutes passed without any sight of an enemy. Some of the soldiers began to break ranks, relaxing along the sides of the road. Places like the hookah bar and assorted restaurants were locked and their guerillas obscured from immediate sight. Locals who encountered the military lied about the presence of adversaries. Some of the officers began to think that it was bad intelligence from high command. Two of the lax troops—young men, neither of whom had reached the age of twenty-two—leaned against the hookah bar's front wall. As they talked, the guerillas, including Aram, heard their conversation.

"Maybe they all left," posited one of them.

"That would not surprise me," stated the other. "My father spoke of a similar sight when he fought in the war for independence."

"Some radio message, right?"

"Yeah, so they say," he added, being audacious enough to remove his helmet and wipe the sweat from his forehead. "Wait a minute! This means you paid attention in history class after all. Color me shocked."

"Well, that part at least. I may be many a thing, friend, but a lukewarm patriot isn't one of them. I know my history overall."

"And your geography—something none of these folk know."

"Yeah, not at all. I heard that their maps don't even have our country on them."

"It's no myth. I don't know if you remember Alia from basic training, but she used to live in one of the monarchies. She told me that not only do they not have us on the map; they claim all the land for that Moab fellow. They've all but declared him king."

"Don't you mean 'president'?" he sarcastically inquired.

"Good one."

"And they always investigate *us* for crimes against humanity. Who has been targeting civilians for the last several months?"

"No need to tell me. I'm just glad I don't fight for them, you know? I could never shoot a child. You couldn't pay me enough."

"Even if it were one of Moab's illegitimate ones?" asked the one soldier, prompting laughter from both of them.

"Okay, that was kind of mean."

"What would you call them?"

"Hey, hey, I don't like to get into politics," he said, putting his helmet back on. "I just want to defend my country."

"That's gradually becoming unacceptable."

"Oh, now, that's where you're wrong. No one in their right mind would ever say that defending our homes is wrong. No government would legislate against it; no global body would forbid it."

"Maybe you're right," conceded the young soldier as he took a look around and gave a deep breath. "Well, we better get the order out to turn the tanks and trucks around. There is nothing to fight here."

Then Aram, full of uncontrollable rage, rushed out of the hookah bar. His very presence caught the attention of the two surprised soldiers, as well as a few others nearby. Seething in every sinew, he shouted, "Die, pig-bloods!" and slapped the center of his chest.

Scene 4

Sherry Francis was an accomplished journalist. Beginning as an intern, she worked her way to the front of the cameras. During her time with the news channel, she had the privilege to interview many notable figures including presidential candidates, big name actors and actresses, members of Congress, cardinals and bishops, activists, thinkers, professors, athletes, best-selling authors, and other household names. Some were interviewed at the station, but most were brought in via satellite.

Five nights a week, Francis was part of two programs. The first she co-anchored with a gentleman, which provided short news updates and often cut to previously recorded stories. The second program, which aired live after the dinner hour, she anchored alone. This latter series centered on interviews with notables rather than reading from prepared rolling text or showing a previously filmed product. It was not an opinion program with her spouting off partisan talking points. An aura of journalistic objectively prevailed overall, with the anchor keeping the bulk of her views to herself.

Camera lights were on, the crew behind the lenses were readying for the return from commercial break. A person in casual wear had rushed onto the stage, double checking to verify that the makeup and liner along the eyes and lips were still effective. Lighting was adjusted for the return to broadcast. Soon, millions of households were going to look at Francis' pretty face, with her fine-trimmed, blonde hair, contact-bearing blue eyes, and artificially rosy cheeks. Her neckline was covered less for modesty and more because someone told her it exposed her age. An appointment with the proper crafter of physical appearance was scheduled for next week. Until then, modesty it was. A man with a headset on began the countdown. Soon, the lights changed, and they were live.

"Welcome back to the program," Francis started. "It is awards season in Hollywood, and many are abuzz about the surprise foreign film hit, *Heaven at Once*. Set in the Middle East, the plot centers on the lives of men who become suicide bombers to resist an oppressive regime. While critically acclaimed, *Heaven at Once* has garnered controversy in many circles for what some consider to be its sympathetic portrayal of terrorism. Here via satellite to answer this claim and more is the film's executive producer, Moab al-Aqsa."

The camera angle changed during Francis' remarks, shifting her from the center of the screen to the left side. Appearing on the right side of the screen was a new live feed, showing Moab's face and upper chest. A boom mic was clearly visible, attached to his right jacket pocket. He smiled as his name was mentioned. The feed was coming several time zones away in his villa. It was very early morning where Moab was located.

"Good morning to you, Mr. al-Aqsa," she said.

"Hello, good evening, Sherry," replied Moab. "How are you?"

"Fine, fine," she responded. "Now, I wanted to talk to you about the reaction the film is getting. A lot of people here in the United

States and in Europe have spoken very highly of it; however, others are concerned about the moral message the film is giving. How do you respond to those concerns?"

"I understand why people may be concerned at first, but it is important to realize that the message of the film is not so much 'terrorism is good' but that 'oppression is bad.' People should do everything they can to resist oppression. That is what the main characters of *Heaven at Once* are doing, and that is what actual members of my people are doing every day in many ways to fight the occupation."

"Understood, Mr. al-Aqsa," said Francis. "However, some believe that, regarding the film and the occupation, there are better ways to fight back. Nonviolent ways."

"We tried nonviolent ways, and they did not work," claimed Moab. "One of our greatest nonviolent activists was a radio figure named Girgash Keniz. In response to his nonviolent activities, he not only lost his radio station; but also, later on, the army shot him dead. We want to live in peace and act peacefully in our resistance, but such options have been denied us—alongside our human dignity, of course."

"I see." She nodded. "So for those of us in the West who may not be familiar with the ongoing conflict, what has it been like to live under the occupation?"

"Absolutely horrible," stated Moab. "The military has put a strain on our lives, which has only gotten worse in recent months. Young men are rounded up solely because of their race or their religion; access to better jobs and homes in the proper territories have been strictly limited; and large numbers of civilians have been slaughtered, again, solely for being minorities. I don't like to use the term, but it is basically genocide. The military is acting just like how the Nazis did decades ago."

"About that, Mr. al-Aqsa: military officials have said that the measures they are taking are meant for national security," Francis countered in a civil tone.

"Are they really, Sherry? Consider the evidence. In the first month of the outbreak of violence, more than six thousand civilians—women and children, mainly—were murdered by the military. Nearly sixty thousand total as of last month. The military has a sick habit of forcing the survivors of their murder sprees to clean up the blood of their dead relatives—usually, young boys. We have plenty of photographic evidence to back up these allegations."

In previous interviews, Moab had to awkwardly hold up the photos that David and Joachim took. However, the news station had gotten copies in advance; and so they were shown, uncensored, on the TV screen for a few seconds each while Moab continued to talk.

"This type of barbarity should not be tolerated by any decent human being. No child—no matter who they are, what god they worship, or the color of their skin—should have to endure the things our children are enduring. The world needs to see these photos; they need to hear more perspectives on this conflict; and they should definitely see *Heaven at Once*."

As the photos disappeared from the screen, the televisions saw again the split screen between Moab and Francis. She faintly smirked at the plug Moab made for the film. Offstage was the man with the headset, giving her the signal to wrap up the interview. Seeing him but not openly acknowledging his message, she addressed Moab.

"One last question before we let you go. As you undoubtedly know, armed forces recently raided a town near where you live called Chaldea. Soon afterward, there were many who claimed that the military performed a massacre of the townsfolk, with as many as five hundred being killed. Are you familiar with those claims; and if so, do you believe them to be valid?"

"It would not surprise me," said Moab without hesitation. "Given their past atrocities, especially those I highlighted tonight, I am surer than sure that they killed hundreds of civilians. Thousands, perhaps. These genocidal actions will only continue as long as the world lets them. They are all responsible."

SCENE 5

Chaldea was surrounded. The army encircled the desert town in less than a half an hour. There was an initial shock from the eruption of hostility. Many of the military became casualties as scores of buildings opened fire upon them. The aims were sporadic, which helped most of those in the open get to safety. Much of the armor was on the main street and easily subdued that backbone of the town. From there, the uniformed troops and their armored aid went through the roads, clearing out whatever enemies appeared. The rattling of gunfire and the occasional pounding explosion became the normative sounds, supplanting the bustle and haggling of the once peaceable inhabitance.

By lunchtime, the army had subjugated most of Chaldea. Guerilla troops with basic training who were more accustomed to attacking unarmed targets found themselves battling a well-trained, professional force. Squads of soldiers with body armor and strict discipline maneuvered around positions—into building corridors, along roofs—and poured fire into all the weak spots. High concentrations of guerillas, like the occasional duplex or restaurant, were leveled by a couple shots from the big guns. Artillery and tanks alike blasted away whole walls, burying any foolish enough to not abandon the doomed edifices. No barrier or building held for long. Meanwhile, thousands of civilians hid in basements while hundreds streamed outside to seek safety under enemy control.

"Do you know what these are?" asked the imam to a six-year-old boy too shy to speak up. The cleric was holding a pair of fake plastic keys, brightly colored and similar to previous items given to other youths.

The big-eyed kid simply smiled, revealing crooked teeth. "Well, these are the keys to the gates of Heaven."

The imam handed the glorified toy to the child, placing them in the youth's right hand and clasping it shut with his own hands. "Hold on to them; you will need them very soon."

They were indoors, with outdoor gunfire heard in the background. There were two other adult men, scruffy in appearance. Each one had a camcorder. They took turns filming things, letting one recharge while the other was used. The facility where they plotted was dark, all lights having been turned off. A diesel generator kept the power going, however, allowing for the cameras to gain battery strength. Through the cracked window, they had optimal angles for the action. One of them looked at the imam and the boy. He was visibly disturbed by the sight but kept any verbal objections to himself.

"Now then, go out there and run toward the first infidel you see," ordered the imam, a hand on each puerile shoulder. "Before you know it, you will be running toward Allah and all his pleasures."

The boy smiled again. A pat on the left shoulder, and the kid was off. Like most of the children who had set off toward the enemy before him, he wore a light-hued vest. Unlike nearly all the others, his was only a vest. The boy went out the back entrance, away from the major road and thus not revealing where he had come from. He skipped and jumped over various piles of rubble and for fun kicked a bunch of shell casings littered over the ground. He was quickly discovered.

"Yakob," said one soldier to his nearest comrade. The man turned around to face his fellow enlisted man. "We got another one."

"It's your turn, Usman."

"Yup."

Usman shouted at the running kid. "Stand down!" He paused and pointed his rifle into the air. "Stand down!" The youth kept running, so he fired a couple of shots into the air. The boy covered his ears at the noise, but still got closer and closer.

Usman cursed and then aimed at the child. He fired a perfect shot into the heart.

Immediately, the boy was thrown backward by the fatal shot and landed onto the rubble. Baffled by the lack of an explosion, he turned to his companion in arms. "Yakob."

"What is it?"

"He didn't blow up."

"A decoy?"

"Maybe."

"But for what, Usman? No one else is coming."

"Maybe they chickened out."

"Maybe," agreed the soldier. "Stay vigilant."

Inside the dark building, the two younger adults examined the footage alongside the imam. After a couple plays and rewinds, the bearded elder grinned, the turning up of his lips visible even through the furry layer of gray. "This is good. This is very good. I think we now have plenty of atrocities to show the world."

"That we do, ya akhi."

"Now, remember, leave the cameras here and take the film and memory cards with you," ordered the imam. "Go with the other refugees from the town. They may search you, but they will be looking for guns, not videos."

"Yes, ya akhi."

David was amidst part of the few remaining blocks that maintained resistance. Outside of his noted clairvoyance in predicting the doom of Chaldea, he offered little else. Planning out strikes against civilian targets or lone military personnel was not on the same plain as organizing a constant defense of territory. Young men occasionally saw him in the streets, running up to him with their questions. Where to find more ammunition, where to rally, what to do when a tank showed up, how much longer until the military overtakes the city. He struggled with every answer, often simply encouraging the youths to keep fighting. He promised no Heaven, but nonetheless asked for sacrifice if need be.

"David! David!" a familiar, feminine voice screamed through the latest wave of bullet and blast.

His view of her was obscured by another cloud of dust from yet another building leveled by the tanks. Esther was wearing a shawl in addition to her other modest attire. David ran toward her without regard to the chaos abounding.

A loud explosion overhead prompted both to bend as they raced toward each other. Tacitly, they agreed to rush to the nearest structure and seek something resembling security.

"Esther! What are you doing away from the inn?"

"My father-in-law told me to run an errand. Then a shell hit the front of the building, blew most of it up."

"Is he dead?"

"I don't know!" she said in great exasperation. "I just know it's our chance to escape. Both of us. Together!"

David paused. He looked down as the sounds of war continued. More structures were leveled, and the number of civilians fleeing to the safety of the military's lines went from hundreds to thousands. Everything was crumbling. Each and every unit he had recruited was being blown away. All that was Chaldea was passing away. Even the vineyards on the outskirts were torn up by the rolling of vehicles and the pitching of tents for the displaced.

"David! We have to go now!"

"Then go we shall," he said upon looking at her desperate sea-green eyes.

She smiled in relief as the two held hands, his left to her right; and they ran down the street.

Ten blocks away from the reunion of David and Esther, Joachim was in charge of eighteen young guerillas holding a line of rubble against the military. Two apartment complexes, once standing on opposite sides of a street, were both destroyed. Hundreds of bricks and pieces of debris were thrown forward into the roadway. It made for decent protection against bullets, allowing for Joachim and his comrades to beat back infantry attacks.

They cheered, and some thanked Allah with each squadron compelled to pull back.

"Keep up the fire! Keep shooting them!" ordered Joachim, who followed his own example and fired his share of rounds at the uniformed enemy. They had their own ruins to hide behind, with rapidly fired bullets chewing up the broken walls.

Soon, the defenders heard the groaning engine among the other martial noises. Soldiers drew back and cleared the way for a sand-colored mechanical creature to slowly venture toward the resistance.

"Throw some grenades! Now! Now!"

Those few that still had such explosives adhered to the shouts. They pulled pins and lobbed them at the machine. Two of them burst in front of the vehicle, causing little damage. However, they kicked up sand and dirt did allow for a brief pause in gunfire as the vision of the armed forces was blurred in the falling earth. Another grenade landed between two of the many wheels, blowing away the track and the wheels. This immobilized the machine. Best of all for the guerillas, a final grenade landed right below the gun tube at the turret. When it blew up, it destroyed the ability of the tank to maneuver or fire the main gun. Its destruction echoed the effects of the old war, reminding a few of that old tank in the desert. More cheers came from the guerillas upon realizing their success.

"Keep up the fight! We will kill them all!" shouted an elated Joachim. The gaiety ceased when two more tanks showed up.

Despite the first one's immobility, the route the vehicle took was wide enough that other tanks were capable of entering the fray. Smiles melted the emergence of fear.

"Grenade! Throw more grenades!"

"That was my last one!" shouted back a teenager on the line. Most were too stunned to move.

Joachim willed himself to run away. He and two others began running as the two gun tubes turned on their working turrets, aimed at the rubble wall, and fire perfect shots that obliterated the line. Joachim and his surviving peers kept running, tossing their weapons to the torn-up ground lest they slow them down.

Another boom from behind and the ground underneath them rose upward. It was like the road itself had become a tidal wave, curling and raising a wall of dirt, cement, and sand. Joachim and his two peers landed hard upon the unbroken ground. As they collected themselves, infantry and tanks moved past the former line of resistance. The two were shaken but unharmed and continued to run away. Joachim, on the other hand, landed especially bad and was semi-conscious. As he regained his full faculties, he saw the armored troops with rifles drawn running toward him. In fear, he desperately kicked away while still on the ground, trying anything and everything to escape.

"This way!" shouted Esther, turning right onto a minor street. She pulled on David's hand, quickly cuing him to follow. They were not totally sure how they were going to leave the ruined city.

David did not know how much military intelligence knew about him. He was sure they knew his name, but could they recognize him also? He was shrewd enough to bar Perziz from ever uploading one of his speeches to social media. Then again, they might have descriptions from the imprisoned. Esther and David agreed to try and find a way to leave Chaldea that did not require vetting from the army.

"The way looks clear!" shouted David in relief, Esther nodding in agreement. It was a challenging trip with proper supplies, but David knew it could be done. It was going to be a hard journey; David was going to make it harder when he planned to inform Esther of his intention to return to the fight. One thing at a time, he thought. First get out, then travel, then let her know. He was already confident. "We are almost out!" he shouted as the desert outskirts looked beautifully vacant. While technically surrounding Chaldea, the growing throngs of refugees required more personnel near main street, providing a temporary opening in the lines. It seemed so romantically ideal.

And then, the explosion happened. The source was unknown. It might have been a shell from either one of the few artillery pieces or from one of the tanks. Then again, it could have been a malfunctioning device from the guerillas. Already four other buildings found themselves seriously damaged from the mishandling of detonators and dynamite. Whatever the reason, the structure to their immediate left exploded, spewing forth tons of bricks, mortar, and other random materials.

Both fell prone to the street. Moments passed, and David rose up. He was covered in a thin layer of debris, mussing his hair and shading his skin and clothes. A few cuts and bruises, but otherwise okay.

"That one was too close," he smartly commented to himself and Esther. "For a moment, I thought we were—" David stopped talking when he saw that she was not moving, her sea-green eyes closed. Several bricks were on top of her body. "Esther? Esther?"

He repeated her name over and over, in greater emotion and more frightened tones. David removed every brick, every little piece of debris. Still, she did not move. Knowing not what to do next, he slowly turned her so that she was on her back. It was then that he saw Esther was still alive but very badly hurt. Shaking intensely as through shivering, her clothes and skin were torn in many places. David released tears from strained eyes. Blood was gushing from multiple places on her chest and left leg.

"Esther, Esther." His shouts became softer and sadder.

She looked at him and tried to form words but was unable to. She was only able to mouth things—maybe words, maybe breaths. David tried to pick her up, to carry her as far as he could. But as Esther's upper half was lifted completely off the ground, the sensitive wounds elicited so much pain as to make Esther scream loudly, tightly shutting her eyes. Realizing that she was immobile, David gently laid her back down. He took her shawl and balled it up to serve as a pillow. He took off his jacket and covered her with it. She begged with her eyes for him to stay.

At first, David obliged. Yet, turning, he saw the approaching troops and tanks. Divided within, he ultimately chose flight. Carefully lifting her upper body to prevent more pain, he embraced her. For her part, she leaned her head into his chest. He kissed her forehead and then carefully lowered her down. After positioning the back of her head onto the makeshift pillow, he took one more look at her, one more look at the oncoming military, and then ran into the desert.

SCENE 6

"What happened to Esther?" inquired Joachim as he and David were sitting on opposite ends of the small table in the study.

"Why are you doing this?" asked an impatient David. His wine glass was empty, but the nearby bottle on the other small table still had some contents within its transparent frame. "It is not as though I've engaged in these evils over the past several years."

"Oh, but you have," countered Joachim, who got up and walked toward the other small table.

David remained seated and turned himself to see where his company was headed.

Three of the fingers on Joachim's right hand gently tapped the printed bill on the tabletop. Looking down at the text, he read aloud, "'A Bill to Advance International Human Rights and Dignity Through the Approval of Divestment and Sanctions.'"

"A beautiful name, don't you think?" said David, beaming with accomplishment. "I basically wrote the whole thing. It will be introduced soon."

"Your hatred is a monster that does not die but simply changes skins," declared Joachim. "What a cruel reason."

"Reason. Reason? Reason! You talk to me about reason. Then, permit me to appeal to your great and glorious reason. Bill or no bill, even you are aware that this has all outgrown me. The movies, the websites, all the videos, ten thousand mosques chanting for their destruction, countless churches and schools cutting off all relations— so much of this is beyond my scope. And you know it."

"You have yet to err in your analysis."

"Then why? Why this? Why this clandestine, little trial? Surely, my death cannot behead this beloved cause. Surely, the monster has escaped Frankenstein. Surely, I cannot, by my lonesome self, close the box of Pandora. So why? Why do this to me?"

"Because of hope," replied Joachim. "Because there is always a chance. A hopeful chance. When word of your demise spreads through the conduits of information, when our people see once again how living by the sword equates to dying by the sword, when this message is proclaimed to the uttermost ends of the earth, people will learn. Maybe legions of them, maybe only thousands, maybe merely hundreds will learn what happens when they follow your wretched path. If even one—yes, even one—of our people decides to turn away from terrorism and to either embrace their separated brethren or to, at the least, pursue peaceful ways of dissent, then it would be as a whole humanity rising against your vile empire. That is what this evening is about. It goes beyond both of us."

"A cute speech," dismissed David.

"What happened to Esther?"

"You keep asking a question you already know the answer to."

"I do not know the whole answer, only portions. Tell me the whole answer; tell me for your own conscience's sake. Tell me, for this is part of what must be done."

David shifted in his chair. His discipline was weakening, his resistance falling away to the resilient Joachim. Silently, he arose from his seat, slightly hunched over from the long hours, looking upward toward the younger man. Joachim was patient, showing little sign of wear from the lengthy eventide debate. David gathered his painful memories from those years ago. He was searching for a way to convey them verbally, hesitant and fragile.

"Did she die?"

"No," David responded, looking down and melancholic.

"Why not?"

"You know why."

"Say it, anyway."

"She did not die," began David, his sadness and anger fusing as one. "She did not die . . . because they saved her." He looked up to Joachim with glassy eyes and angered expression. "Is that what you wanted to hear? Then, I will say it again. They saved her. They found her after I ran away like a coward. They took her to a medical facility, along with scores of other wounded civilians. She survived."

"And then what happened?"

"I . . . I tried to see her again. In the hospital. It turned out . . . it turned out that the military did not know what I looked like. They knew my name, so I changed it."

"David al-Nassery."

"Yes," nodded David, fighting back a wellspring of emotion as he neared the most painful memory of them all. "I got into the hospital. I went to her. Even with all the . . . even with all the bandages and scars, she was still so beautiful. She told me she was happy to see me alive. She really did." A tear escaped his right eye as he continued to look blankly forward, technically at the wall of books behind Joachim but not intentionally so.

"Then . . . then, she said . . . she said . . . " Another tear escaped from the right eye. As he continued, a tear fell from the left eye as well. "She said she wanted nothing to do with me. She was done with me. She never wanted to see me again." David looked again at Joachim. "Is that what you wanted? You wanted me to confess my wrongs. And that I did. Now I confess to you that the woman I loved the most never wants to see me again."

"Why did she make this conclusion?"

"The cause."

"That is my point, the point you suppress with wine and banter, with rage and anger. All those still free and among the living who most knew you have left you."

"Truly," agreed David, wiping away the last of the fleeing tears from his eyes. "She wants nothing to do with me. You want me to die. And all else is gone. Only the cause remains."

"A cause that has reaped great suffering upon not just them but also your own. The people of Chaldea, the mothers of the occupied region, all those you sent to die because of your primitive enmity."

David was silent. He slowly turned away from Joachim. A few sniffles from his dreary mood were heard as he buttoned up his shirt. Raising his collar, he put back on the tie he wore during the festive part of the evening. Upon tightening the fashionable noose, he put down the flaps of his collar. Then, he took hold of the jacket he had previously laid upon his chair. He put the garment on, pushing his arms through the sleeves. Buttoning the item to secure it to his body, he turned again to face his company.

"And then, I came here," explained David. "Moab funded the trip. He told me I earned it. And he agreed with my latest strategy to destroy them."

"Appeal to the West," noted Joachim. "Come to them as a helpless—yet likeable—refugee, someone oppressed and afflicted solely for his race."

"As I said near the onset of our little dialogue, Joachim, they value diversity above all else in this time and place."

"And you used the Western political system to attack them from here."

"Yes, indeed."

"As if all of your crimes were not enough, as if there were not enough of us and them who have suffered because of your actions, you drag into suffering still more of the human race," commented Joachim, stern and upright. "For the many who will flee their lands because of war and of oppression and of persecution, for the many who desperately seek safety far away from their ravaged homes, for those sincerely in need and those sincerely helpless, the great majority of all of those who flee to this land and like it. Now the vile, the xenophobe, the hater of his fellow man—these and more will be able to use your cruel life as justification to fuel a hatred as Satanic as the one you bear. They will cite you when they justify disobeying God's command to love the neighbor and the stranger; they will reference your life for their particular hate. Esther was right to reject you."

David wanted to say something. He wanted to issue a retort. However, he found himself unable to. He was starting to accept the charges laid against him. Bowing his head before Joachim, he faintly nodded.

The guest was somewhat surprised, but he kept such emotion from proper view.

"I wanted you to survive, Joachim. I held out hope. You were my best soldier, my second-in-command, and like a son. I see you have survived in bodily form only. You said I had nothing, and you are right. All I have done is inflict suffering and bigotry upon the world. Even here in a land of new futures, I continue to stain the air. There are nights, Joachim, nights when I want to end it because I know I can never be with her. There are nights when I realize just how wrong I was because I know that I rejected her before she rejected me. I chose terrorism over her. I chose unbridled hate over true love." David lumbered over to the small table with the gun.

Joachim followed, circling around him so that he was between the party host and the lone door that led to the exit. David continued to look down. "Tonight reminds me of how much wrong I have dedicated myself to throughout my life. Whenever I think of Esther, I am painfully reminded of that again."

"Then, will you do it?" asked Joachim, who pushed the pistol several inches across the tabletop toward David.

There was a quiet deep enough that the few active vehicles outside at that hour were heard. David glanced at Joachim as the visitor's right hand let go of the weapon. David examined the modern gun, its black frame and solid form. He touched the item with his left hand, fingers lightly dancing upon the weapon. With a deep breath, his fingers gripped the gun; and his face became enraged.

"No," David declared, pushing the weapon back across the small table. "I will not do it. I will not give you the pleasure of a pitiful end." David smiled, his confidence returning.

Joachim remained steadfast, evidently preparing for the oncoming deluge.

"I will not do it. Never. I have far too much to live for. The expectation of a new ally, the growing influence in the West . . . all of this and more. Do I regret what I did in the old country? Not enough. Not enough to end it all. Pain I have endured, but it was pain that was worth it just to see that disgusting, subhuman race suffer even more. Weeping over their dead children, moaning as the bullets and the bombs tear them to shreds! Yes, Joachim, I embrace it all with pride. And there is nothing—*nothing*—you can do about it.

"What now? Are you going to shoot me? Then, shoot me! Make me a martyr, Joachim. Give the divestment bill the grease of my blood, so it can spin even faster through Parliament and through the world! For as I was able to deceive Islamic civilization to follow my every hatred, so shall I deceive Christian civilization into doing the same! And it shan't be that hard, either. After all, it wasn't that long ago that some of their polities were quite supportive of exterminating those pig-bloods and their plague of a species. I will revive such a mentality. *That* is the future, my apostate friend. And when I have succeeded, I will have purged the human race of that vile cancer once and for all time. I will not rest until every last one of them is *dead*!"

At that moment, David was his truest self. The layers of civility, deception, and eloquence fell away to reveal his innermost desires. In contrast to earlier in the discussion, when the otherwise civil David was taken to shock over his own outbursts, this time he was accepting of the spirit and letter of his rhetoric. He breathed hard as before but this time in accomplishment. He grinned at his peer, overwhelmed with confidence.

Joachim maintained a professional proper figure, calmly addressing his contemporary. "So, you refuse to recant?"

"Their blood be on me and my people," David defiantly stated.

"Then, congratulations, David Shapsdale . . . You just killed yourself," said Joachim, bringing confusion to David's expression.

Joachim loosened his tie, letting the knot drop a few inches from the top button of his outer shirt. He then undid the second button from the top and the third button from the top. While his left hand held his tie and one of the shirt sides, Joachim used his right hand to go inside the outer shirt and pull out a white wire. He held the thin line with a hooked right index finger.

David's eyes fluttered in surprise; his whole body began to warm up, and some sweat escaped his pores.

Still looking at his company, Joachim's left hand let go of the tie and the shirt side, with his thumb and index finger pressing against something immediately behind the top button. Joachim bowed his head, with his chin almost touching his chest. David stood in front of him, hunched over and dumbfounded.

"Did you get all that?" spoke Joachim into the device, located behind the top button. A sound of static was heard, and then a voice answered.

"Every word," replied General Ruth Greenberg, seated inside an unsuspecting van parked two blocks from the apartment complex. "We will be up there soon."

With the second statement, Greenberg exhaled with humble accomplishment. Her hair had grayed since the day that Chaldea was stormed. Turning away from her laptop and the recording system that backed up her statement, she saw six people loading their weapons and putting on chest protectors. Among them was Corporal Shiri Dahan Pirani, who meekly smiled at her seated superior. There were also three journalists in civilian clothes, brought in to report on the unintended confessions of a fugitive.

Within the study, Joachim placed the wire back inside his clothing. The hue of the wire, the undershirt, and the outer shirt had been as one, securing the camouflage. He kept his gaze upon a disoriented David while buttoning up his shirt, tightening his tie, and then smoothing out the tie and shirt with a few brushes of the hand. The two stood there silently for a couple of moments, David still attempting to grasp the revelation. He was sedate, his tone more ponderous than frightful.

"So, that's how you survived," said David, realizing at that moment that when Joachim first went to the proper territory following the downfall of Chaldea, he did so as a prisoner and converted while in captivity.

Joachim simply nodded.

David looked back down at the firearm on the small table. It seemed like the perfect time for revenge. But then it occurred to him that his guest was one for advanced planning. He looked back up to Joachim. "Empty?"

Joachim nodded again.

David nodded back. After a few seconds of peace, Joachim turned without taking the unloaded weapon with him and began to walk toward the exit.

"Will I see you again?" asked David as an afterthought. He was unsure why he sent out this query.

It stopped Joachim. However, the younger man did not utter a word; neither did he turn back. He kept walking. David looked back at the table; not at anything in particular, just in existential angst, still piecing together what had happened.

Joachim got to the door at a calm walk, unlatched the two bolts and turned the knob. Opening it, he walked out, letting the swinging door shut behind him.

In the hallway, Joachim went to the row of hangers on the one side. His was the only jacket remaining on the hooks. After putting it on, he took hold of his fedora. It was the only hat on the shelf. Taking hold of the top of the fedora, he was initially going to put it upon his head. Yet midway through the transfer from board to head, he stopped. Joachim changed his mind and placed the fedora flatly on his chest. In the reverent posture, he calmly walked toward the stairway as though in solemn procession.

Outside of the apartment complex, the double doors on the back of the van swung open. Six people, all armed and armored, rushed out of the Trojan horse. Shiri led them as they entered the evening exterior. Four others in civilian clothing joined them. They had been grouped into pairs, each one walking about either side of the roadway that dead-ended into the street next to the main entrance of the apartment complex. They were armed with pistols and wore chest protectors underneath their jackets. The ten ventured onward, making rapid progress across the one street, and filed onto either side of the front entrance. Shiri directed the one who specialized in picking locks to get to the door. The spectacled man took out his equipment and made short work of the basic lock for the main portal. Door opened, Shiri led the strike force into the hallway and up the stairs that led to the penthouse.

Inside the study, David was alone. He walked over to the small table that had the bottle and the printed bill. He came to the spot holding his wine glass. Placing the goblet onto the tabletop, he took hold of the bottle. Tipping it, he once again filled the bowl of the glass. Placing the bottle on the wet rings that developed on the printed bill, David put his left hand into his shirt pocket and removed the pill. Suspending it just above the top of the glass, he used two fingers from each hand to crack it open, allowing its fatal contents to enter the small, fermented pool. He took hold of the stem of the glass, raising it up so that it was at his eye level. Objectively, he already knew what was within it. Yet only then did he subjectively appreciate it, causing him much anxiety. He flinched; he breathed hard; he fought all his inherent urges for survival and the anger at being tricked.

Joachim was nearing the head of the stairs when he caught sight of them. He heard their rumblings seconds earlier, but now they were on the stairs before him. An intense glare came from Corporal Pirani, her Uzi held outward. On either side of her were the others. They were a varied population. Two had fair skin and blue eyes; six had darker features; and another was of African descent. Two wore glasses; another two wore contacts. One was a diabetic, another allergic to penicillin. Three females and seven males, aged between early twenties and late thirties. They also beheld in ferocity the calm Joachim, holding his fedora to his chest. Gritting her teeth, Pirani waved off Joachim with the Uzi, twice using the gun to point to her right side. Joachim nodded and shifted his direction to walk to his left. As he descended the stairway, they jogged up the stairs on either side.

Joachim did not bother to stop or look behind him. He knew what was going to happen.

Standing at the small table with the printed bill, David repositioned his empty wine glass upon the tabletop. He took hold of the bottle and tipped it to fill the bowl. After the contents filled a third of the glass, the thin stream became a few drips. Shaking it a little to get the very last of it, David saw that the bottle was spent.

He considered it appropriate. After setting the bottle down, he took hold of the stem and made a circular motion with his hand, causing the scarlet drink to spin around within the bowl. He then lifted the drink toward his face and bowed his head to have his nose hover just above the top. When David inhaled the fresh smell of the prized wine, a flood of memories abounded. Lifting his head up, his eyes remained closed in nostalgia until opened by the jerked opening of the door. He did not see this event, as his back was to the entryway.

The foreign soldiers in uniform and plain clothes fanned out, each aiming a firearm of some type at him. Pirani and two others had Uzis; the four who had been waiting outside of the van had side-arms held with both hands; and the remainder had assault rifles. David stood there in his formal attire. He stood still in his white button-up shirt; navy blue dinner jacket and tie; and light-hued khakis, black socks, and black Oxford shoes. The ten semi-surrounded the man, who held a wine glass with his left hand. Pirani declared the usual statements of arrest, noting the many charges he faced.

David slowly shifted around to eventually face the corporal. They were only seven feet away from each other. He was calm, then jovial. Slowly, that sadistic smile, that expression of happy horror, came upon his face. David lifted his glass as though to toast his newly arrived company.

They each looked at him as a figure of great insanity. He carefully looked at each of them while the glass remained high. His smile stubborn and unbroken, a thin line of blood began to exit from the right corner of his mouth. Then another line of blood began to flow out of his left nostril. As the blood began to escape from the other corner of his mouth, David began to shake and stumble, falling back upon the small table. His free hand attempted to balance him by taking hold of the table corner; but it did no good as he fell forward, losing his grip on the glass. It shattered upon the floor.

Pirani ordered the two with the most medical knowledge to see to David, who was on his back, writhing in anguish. Blood was flowing from his mouth and both nostrils, flooding his throat. The two put their weapons on the floor and descended to the side of David, whose left leg was constantly kicking while his outstretched right arm flailed about. They did what they could, removing his tie and tearing open his outer shirt. The kicking started to lessen; the moving of the arm weakened. The fingers on his right hand kept bending and unbending with weaker and weaker intensity. And then, they stopped curling. The leg stopped kicking, and the heart stopped beating. One of the two soldiers by his side checked for the vital signs. As Pirani approached, the one who checked the signs turned to look up at his superior and shook his head. The other confirmed the expiration.

All ten of them neared the corpse of David Shapsdale. Their weapons were lowered. They stood there in silence. As they gathered around the body with much emotion, Shiri searched her pants pocket. She quickly located the item. Those who did not look at the deceased beheld their superior officer as she took an old, light green pacifier and tossed it underhand onto the corpse. It landed upon the chest of the dead and then rolled down the side, positioned between his torso and left arm. While the others discerned many thoughts standing over the body, Shiri lived in peace.

Scene 7

Michael Bradford and his wife, Megan, stood outside of the apartment complex. They were still in their proper attire from the party. He was wearing an overcoat in addition to his dinner jacket while she had on a winter jacket and also a shawl covering her arms. Stockings under the flowing dress also helped her retain heat during the cold night. They spent some of the time waiting outside of the main entrance, some of the time inside their car at the nearby garage, and some walking around the adjacent blocks. Neither expected the evening to be so long, but they were prepared nonetheless. When Megan noticed the small group of armed people entering the building, she alerted her husband; and the two exited their parked automobile. There they waited for news of what happened. To keep awake, they had engaged in cups of coffee and intellectual banter.

"You know," said Michael after a period of silence, holding a warm coffee that was sheltered inside a plastic cup with a top. "They say that many people die around this time, four or 4:30 in the morning."

"Really?" asked Megan, who had a similar drink in her hands.

"Yes," stated Michael. "As I understand, many—if not most—of those who die of natural causes pass away right about now."

"Interesting," she said, as she, like Michael, kept most of her ocular attention centered on the main entrance of the apartment complex. Both were about twelve feet from the door.

"More than interesting; I actually find it quite providential."

"Providential?" asked Megan, briefly steering her gaze toward her husband.

"Yes, providential," began Michael, who made his points while maintaining a look at the door. "Think for a moment about what happens to those who have a loved one die between four and 4:30 in the morning. When they leave the hospital, or the bedroom, or wherever, they enter a world that looks as they feel—bleak, cold, dark, and dreary. For that time, the world agrees with them that there is only tragedy and sorrow, that death is all there is, and that nothing more is there for them to look forward to." Michael's solemn tone dramatically changed as he continued to make his point. "But then, it happens."

"What happens?"

"The sunrise, of course! Not long after this dread period shows itself, a new one appears. A new era emerges—one of warmth, comfort, clarity, richness, and security, of light and new beginning. When that warming, pleasant orb ascends over the horizon, why, the radiance is so great, you cannot even look at it directly. That is when the beautiful epiphany finally arrives. The realization that despite that time of darkness, there is always a better time coming. Life goes on; hope endures; there is more to it all than just suffering and hardship. There is something better, and it is always almost here. The epiphany is this: that no matter how brutal, how cruel, how hopeless, how vile, how savage, how disturbing . . . every night eventually surrenders . . . to day."

Megan was strangely moved by his remarks.

Michael continued. "At this moment, people all over our nation are beginning that cycle of epiphany, right now, between four and 4:30 in the morning."

Megan checked her phone. "I actually have five 'til seven."

"Well," bashfully spoke her husband, "you get the idea."

While Megan looked away from the entrance to give Michael a wry smile, the door moved and out of the hallway came Joachim, fedora held to his chest. He seemed oblivious to the presence of the Bradfords, even though they were only a few feet to his left.

Michael noticed Joachim and drew his attention. "Hey, stranger. Stranger! Stranger!"

Joachim halted and turned to face the elderly gentleman who had tipped off authorities from abroad to David Shapsdale, leading them to once again get the willful help of the reformed terrorist lieutenant. He had a serene expression as Michael spoke.

"Was it really him?"

"Yes, yes, it was," replied Joachim, with Megan and Michael exchanging comments amongst themselves.

"Wow."

"Unbelievable."

"Unthinkable!"

"Beyond amazing!"

"*The* David Shapsdale."

"In our city!"

"In our very presence!"

"I never would have guessed."

"He was a master at good deception," acknowledged Joachim.

"Out of curiosity," queried Michael, "why did it take so long? Seemed like a simple matter of identification to me."

"Well," began Joachim, still holding the fedora to his chest, "David and I had a bit of a theological disagreement that needed to be resolved."

"Theological?" asked Megan.

"Yes. You see, David kept insisting that death was, as he put it, 'the greatest inevitability.' I knew he was wrong."

Both Bradfords laughed in dissenting amusement.

"Are you sure about that, stranger?" asked Michael.

"Indeed, last I checked, the death rate was 100 percent."

"True," noted Joachim, "for the typical person, the moment they are conceived, they are destined to die. Indeed, there are good odds that every person who is drawing breath at this very hour will someday be shoveled into a grave."

The Bradfords both nodded at these points.

Then, Joachim countered their perceptions with truth. "However, there will come a generation, that last generation, the one that sees the fulfillment of all things, the end of days, and the destruction of death itself. Among their number, millions, if not more, will never taste death. Therefore, death is only the second greatest inevitability."

Joachim placed his fedora on his head and was about to leave, but Michael waved at him and spoke up. "Stranger! One last question before you go. If death is only the second greatest inevitability, then what is the greatest inevitability?"

Joachim al-Dunya, without any evidence of doubt in his heart or in his mind or in his soul or in his strength, smiled at the elderly couple, and replied with the same confidence the Bradfords had of the coming sunrise.

"Judgment."

Not All Shall Sleep.

Not All Shall Be Saved.

Not All Shall Be Damned.

Yet All Shall Be Judged.

About the Author

Michael Gryboski was born and raised in the Washington, D.C. metropolitan area. He graduated from George Mason University with a bachelor of arts and then a master's, both in history. In addition to writing fiction, Michael also writes news articles for a living. Michael would rather be correct than widely accepted.

More Ambassador International titles by Gryboski:

The Enigma of Father Vera Daniel

Memories of Lasting Shadows

A Spiral into Marvelous Light

Follow Michael Gryboski at the following links:

www.facebook.com/MichaelCGryboski

www.instagram.com/michaelgryboski

www.x.com/MichaelGryboski

JAKE TYSON

VIGILANTE'S LIGHT

After his rescue from guerillas in Venezuela, Gideon finds himself with super-abilities, result from genetic engineering during his capture. When he returns home, he finds his beloved city in shambles and torn apart by crime. The police are understaffed and most do not care about the poor side, The Brooks. Gideon becomes a vigilante to protect his city and uses his newfound abilities. But he learns that being a vigilante comes with a price.

Betty is sure that Ida Lou does not belong in their church when the woman shows up to the Good Friday service with her small dog in tow. But before she knows what's happening, Betty—along with the other women of the WUFHs (Women United For Him)—is pushed into helping the woman. God works in mysterious ways—and through ordinary people. The town of Prosper is about to experience some drama—and it all starts with a dog who comes to church.

WHO BROUGHT THE DOG TO CHURCH?

a novel

TRACY L. SMOAK

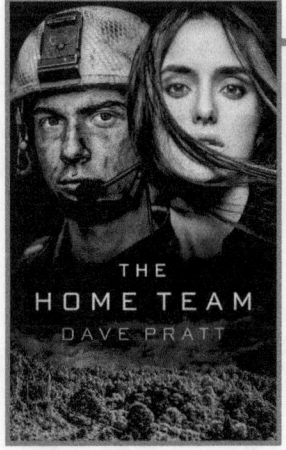

THE HOME TEAM

DAVE PRATT

Sam Anthem has always been a team player, leading his Home Team on secret missions around the world. When he is forced on a vacation, he is introduced to a former covert ops soldier-turned pastor. But the vacation takes a turn when the Home Team comes under attack. As the team fights to stay alive against an unknown adversary, Sam begins to wonder if there is more to life than just the job. With his life on the line, Sam must decide between the job or his newfound faith and possible love.